Also by Tim Peake and Steve Cole

Swarm Rising

TIM PEAKE
and Steve Cole

HODDER CHILDREN'S BOOKS

First published in Great Britain in 2022 by Hodder & Stoughton

1 3 5 7 9 10 8 6 4 2

A CIP catalogue record for this book is available from the British Library.

ISBN 978 1 444 96087 7

Typeset in Garamond by Avon DataSet Ltd, Alcester, Warwickshire

Printed and bound in Great Britain by Clays Ltd, Elcograf S.p.A.

The paper and board used in this book are made from wood from responsible sources.

Hodder Children's Books
An imprint of
Hachette Children's Group
Part of Hodder & Stoughton Limited
Carmelite House
50 Victoria Embankment
London EC4Y 0DZ

An Hachette UK Company
www.hachette.co.uk

www.hachettechildrens.co.uk

TP – *For Aiden and Ruth, your stars will always
shine brightly*

SC – *For Tobey, as you face the future*

THEY'RE HERE . . .

When the alien Swarm arrived on Earth, they weren't travelling in spacecraft. They came at the speed of light, a signal in code, a hive of intelligence. When they got here, they found an Earth in trouble: its air and water poisoned, its climate warming fast.

Their solution was frighteningly simple – remove humans. Upload the entire human intelligence into digital form and let the planet recover.

But then the Swarm's agents made contact with two teenagers – Danny Munday and Jamila al-Sufi – who helped persuade them that humans should be given one more chance. That people can be a force for good. That we can put things right.

And that's when the Swarm made a terrible mistake.

When they departed, they left behind the faintest traces

of Swarm technology. The tiniest whispers of alien code that, in the wrong hands, could destroy the entire planet.

Advanced technology has brought so much good to our civilisation but there is always the danger that greedy people will abuse it for their own ends – or meddle in things they do not fully understand.

You see, in the eyes of an advanced intelligence, humans are little more than toddlers. And toddlers shouldn't be allowed to play with dangerous technology . . .

FIVE YEARS FROM NOW . . .

CHAPTER ONE
POWERFUL SECRETS

Did you ever go to cheer on your best mate when she was trying out for athletics club? Did you ever clap and whoop for her as she sprinted over the hurdles, ignoring the looks you got off the cool kids?

And did you ever then see that best mate sprint straight *through* the final hurdle like it wasn't even there?

I'm thinking not.

As for me – Danny Munday, watching on a Wednesday with my eyes out on stalks – yep, you guessed. That's what happened to me. I saw my best mate Jamila's legs do the impossible. Straight. Through. The. Metal. Barrier.

Mr Sunaki, the games teacher, looked mind-blown. 'That was great work, Jamila! I didn't even see you jump that last one . . .'

Jamila looked as confused as I did. 'Well, I couldn't have run straight through it . . . could I?'

'Right.' Mr Sunaki blinked. 'I guess it was a trick of the light.'

Some trick, I thought, with a sick feeling in my stomach. I reckoned I might have another explanation.

Because me and Jamila have form with weird stuff. As you're going to find out.

'It's the high jump for you now, Jamila,' said Mr Sunaki.

'Sir, no!' Flustered, I stood up. 'That's not fair – she didn't do anything! I mean, nothing weird or . . .' I trailed off as I realised Mr Sunaki was looking at me oddly. 'Um. Right?'

'I meant, she'll be trying out for the high jump, Danny,' he said, and tutted. 'Quick breather and I'll see you over there, Jamila, OK?'

I was left standing red-faced, trying not to wilt under the withering stares from the cool kids.

Jamila jogged over to join me, holding up two sarcastic thumbs. 'Way to boost my rep, Danny-boy!'

Her thick black hair was pushed up in a scruffy ponytail, bouncing as she panted for breath. She grinned, genuine this time. 'Anyway, did you see my mega performance? What did you think?'

My smile was less certain. 'Er . . .'

'Let me help you out as usual.' She rubbed her chin, mock thoughtful. 'I think you saw *greatness*.'

'You felt all right running then?' I said. 'Nothing weird? Only, I thought I saw . . .'

' "Greatness",' Jamila insisted. 'That's the word you're groping for.'

She was wrong. I had a word; a word that was ready-made and good to go on the tip of my tongue. A word you wouldn't find in any dictionary. Not on this planet at least.

But I bit my tongue cos I was officially banned from saying that word – and a whole lot like it – out loud. Me and Jamila, we made a pinky swear five months ago: Never Talk About What Happened When *They* Came.

'We can't keep going over stuff in the past,' Jamila had decided. 'It was so intense, so out there. We have to bury it or we'll never move forward with our normal lives.'

Well, she was moving forward now all right – straight through solid metal hurdles. My stomach felt all tight and tickly with worry at what her 'greatness' might mean.

'You went really fast,' I said. 'Jam, are you . . . feeling OK?'

'I'm feeling awesome,' Jamila said and struck a dramatic pose. 'Now I've got to do the high jump, then show what I can do in one of the throwing events.'

'Throwing up?' I suggested.

'Throwing the hammer,' said Jamila. 'At your head. So watch . . . out.' She swayed suddenly and blinked. 'Ow. Feels like someone's already lobbed a hammer at my skull.'

'Maybe you should sit down,' I said, feeling more and more worried. 'Come on, sit down with me.'

'Don't be so needy,' Jamila teased. 'I want to do well. I can do this. My mum is always moaning I don't do enough sports.'

'You mean gaming and stuffing Doritos with me doesn't count?'

'Strange but true,' said Jamila. 'Mum wants me doing something constructive.'

'Constructive!' I snorted. 'Jam, you basically saved the planet from . . .'

'Zip it, Munday!' Jamila was suddenly fierce and all up in my face. 'We agreed. No more talking about *that*.'

'I'm only saying—'

'Well, don't, OK?' She turned and stalked crossly away to where Mr Sunaki waited in front of the squashy blue crash mats. The horizontal bar had been placed in front of them, maybe a metre-forty high. I knew Jamila was good at PE and had great balance – most nights she secretly crossed from her house next door, out through her bedroom window and in through mine with a swing around the drainpipe in between – but I had no idea how she would get on with the high jump.

Mr Sunaki gestured vaguely to the bar as he checked his clipboard. 'Are you ready, Miss al-Sufi?'

Jamila didn't wait for him to be ready. As she neared the bar she broke into a half-run.

And then she broke the laws of physics.

She jumped and twisted in mid-air as she threw herself backwards over the bar. But her heels were going to strike it. Jamila saw and suddenly she jerked higher into the air, as if pulled on invisible elastic. She cleared the bar by about ten centimetres and kept travelling through the air until she overshot the crash mats and landed face down on the grass with a thud. The sound drew the attention of the cool kids who gave a slow hand clap.

'Jam!' I yelled and sprinted over to where she'd fallen. I might have made the athletics team myself if Mr Sunaki had been watching. But he was crouched beside Jamila by now, helping her sit up. She had a trickle of blood from her left nostril and looked woozy, out of it.

I pulled a tissue from my pocket and handed it to her. 'Gross,' she said, but took it anyway.

'Are you all right, Jamila?' Mr Sunaki looked shell-shocked. 'That jump . . . I never saw . . . are you . . . I mean . . . ?'

'I don't feel so good,' Jamila said, rubbing her head.

'You're lucky you didn't hurt yourself worse. You fell pretty hard.'

'I'll be OK in a minute, sir,' Jamila insisted.

'Nope. Your trial ends here. We should get you home but the bus isn't due to leave for another forty-five minutes.' Mr Sunaki pondered. 'Can your mum collect you?'

'She'll be taking my older brother into work,' Jamila said.

Mr Sunaki looked at me. 'Danny, your parents . . . ?'

'Since you ask, my dad's an astrophysicist who lives in Hawaii since the divorce and my mum's a radio astronomer who spends most of her life working with the Lovell Telescope at Jodrell Bank, so basically, no, not a chance in hell.' That's what I wanted to say. Instead I just wrinkled up my face and shook my head.

'We could call a taxi,' I suggested. Our playing fields are three miles from the main school campus – we share them with another academy – so we couldn't just walk back home. 'The bus will take ages.'

'Let me see what I can do,' said Mr Sunaki. 'Danny, take Jamila to the main gate – there's a bench there.'

'Hear that, Jam? A bench. We're spoiling you.'

I helped her stand and whispered in her ear. 'Do you feel sick? Stomach cramps? Burning heat in your veins?'

She gave me a sharp look as she realised what I was driving at. 'Danny, please, stop it.'

'Don't pretend stuff isn't happening,' I told her. 'Why won't you just talk about it?'

'Because I can't!' she hissed, pushing me away. 'You have no idea what it was like for me – trapped in the Internet without a body, trying to hold it together while my brain was blown about like smoke through the Wi-Fi. And all because of *them* . . .' Her grin from before was gone. She looked exhausted. Unhappy.

I didn't answer. For all I'd been going on at her to talk about things, I suddenly found I had no idea what to say.

It's tough, you know? When you've literally saved the whole world but you can never tell anyone cos no one would *ever* believe you. Me and Jam, we saved it from a hive mind of alien superbrains who thought the Earth would be a better place without human beings. Obvs we didn't do it alone – one of the Swarm helped us.

Her name was Adi. A-D-I: short for Alien Digital Intelligence.

And in order to help us, first Adi had to *change* us.

Let me put it like this: you know when you do your homework on the computer? It exists as a digital thing. You can copy it, download it, edit it, email it, send it pretty much anywhere. Or you can print it out as a hard copy so it's not digital any more – it's a physical thing you can touch.

Now swap out the homework for the one thing even scarier – *aliens*. Imagine aliens that exist as digital intelligences without form or mass. Aliens that can send themselves through space at the speed of light, like radio waves. When they reach a planet with advanced technology, they can get inside things like the Internet, copy themselves, spread all over the world. And imagine if they could create special machines to print themselves as flesh and blood . . . turn into physical beings with special powers that make them more than human. Powers to warp the world around them.

Powers that could, say, make a hurdle transparent or

bend solid metal just by thinking about it.

I'm sure you get where this is going.

Creepy as, right?

I could tell you so much more about the Swarm but I don't want to overload your puny Earthling brains (joke!) with backstory all at once. All you need to know right now is that when you turn a human body digital and then turn it back to normal, you get . . . complications.

And, trust me, I take complications to the max.

CHAPTER TWO
SOMEPLACE TO CRASH

'It's OK, Jam,' I said, as if saying that would magically make it true. But if nothing else, it did seem to bring a bright white minibus nosing into the car park.

A woman in her mid-twenties with dyed red hair sat at the wheel and she called to me as her window slid open. 'Excuse me.' She smiled, revealing teeth in train-track braces. 'You kids need a ride home? One of you not feeling so good?'

'That's right,' I said, jumping up from the bench. 'Good old Mr Sunaki. Come on, Jam. Not quite a taxi but it'll do.'

'Maybe if I think hard enough I can turn it *into* a taxi,' Jamila muttered as I helped her on board. 'That's the kind of stunt you pulled when *you* had alien juice inside you, right?'

'The more you use that alien juice, the more it hurts,' I told her. 'As I reckon you're finding out.'

Jamila isn't an alien, obvs. She's the most *human* human being I know. But, as I've been hinting so mysteriously, thanks to those aliens, the two of us were turned into digital versions of ourselves and later reprinted. I came out with genes full of alien energy – *energenes*. And those energenes gave me powers you can barely imagine. I could move through solid objects, I could change matter around me. The powers hurt me, made me feel sick, and it didn't take long to burn right through them. I was left normal again.

Jamila stayed digital for way longer than me, though, and was reprinted from a different machine. A more sophisticated machine. *So* sophisticated I thought it had brought Jamila back to real life exactly as she had been.

But what if it hadn't?

What if she'd come out with energenes too, or something even more powerful – and now they were ready to break out?

I helped Jamila into a seat halfway back and settled

in beside her. 'Look, Jam,' I said, 'maybe this is all a fuss about nothing. But if anything *is* up with you, I'm here to help, OK?' I glanced up to find the driver looking back at me.

'There's bad traffic on the A34,' she said. 'I'll take the back way into Didsbury.'

'Thanks,' I said. Jamila didn't say anything. Her eyes were closed and she was sound asleep. I felt a twinge of envy at the thought that Jam might be coming into powers. I'd known that thrill myself, and the fear that had come with it. But those feelings had faded and gone, and now I mostly only remembered the awesomeness of doing the impossible . . .

Except for when I saw Jam suffer.

'How's your friend?' asked the driver, glancing over her shoulder. 'How're you doing, Jam?'

'Jamila,' I said automatically. 'Only I call her Jam.'

'Sorry,' said the driver. '*Jamila* looks really rough.'

'She'll be fine,' I insisted, but I had to agree. Her face was wet with sweat and there were funny flutterings under her skin, like her muscles were having a party while she slept.

'I really don't want her throwing up in here,' the driver said sternly. 'Keep a close eye. I'll be ready to pull over.'

'Don't hurl, Jam,' I whispered in her ear and she stirred. 'Repeat after me: I will not throw up. I will not throw—'

'The hammer,' Jamila said, her eyes snapping open. 'I was meant to throw the hammer.' She stared round in confusion. 'I'm never gonna get on the team if I don't do well in the hammer.'

'That's not happening today, Jam,' I told her. But Jamila had bunched her fist like she was really holding something. Then, eyes closed, still in her seat, she started swinging it over her head like she was Thor about to throw mighty Mjölnir. 'Jam, I'm pretty sure Mr Sunaki would say that's not the way to . . .'

I trailed off. Wispy trails of sparky blue energy were dancing in the circles Jamila was making with her hand, like she was a witch conjuring a spell. My stomach sank like a counterweight to my heart, which was rising up into my mouth. I looked at the driver and found her watching the light show instead of the traffic.

She didn't look scared. There was awe in her eyes. She was transfixed.

'*Look out!*' I yelled. The minibus had strayed from the lane into the path of an oncoming truck. The truck's horn blasted as Driver Girl slammed on the brakes and yanked hard on the wheel. We went screeching off to the left.

And Jamila opened her hand holding the imaginary hammer.

A hole smashed open in the side of the minibus and the window above exploded. I thought we were going to overturn with the force of the impact, but Driver Girl brought the minibus back under control. I saw we had left the main road for a tarmacked lane on an industrial estate.

But we were still barrelling along really fast.

'Stop the bus!' I shouted.

'I've lost control,' the driver bawled back, wrestling with the gearbox and pumping the pedals, trying to bring down our speed. 'Nothing's working!'

We were heading straight for the wall of a warehouse.

'Get ready!' the driver shouted.

Ready to do what, I thought. Crash? I checked my seatbelt was buckled and then turned to Jamila. 'Wake up!' I shook her by the shoulders. Her eyes had rolled back in her head and I could see nothing but the whites. 'Stop this!'

She didn't respond. I could hardly hear myself over the giant roar from the engine. A wall of red bricks reared up ahead of us like a tsunami ready to smash into us with fatal force.

'For God's sake, Jam,' I yelled in her face. '*Please!*'

Jamila was shaking in my grip. I screwed up my eyes.

Then the sound of the engine stopped dead. A wave of heat thrummed through me.

'*Incredible!*' our driver breathed and I could hear wonder spark from every syllable.

It was like time had slowed around us. A hole opened up in the brickwork, like a tunnel, allowing us to pass. And the minibus rolled quietly through it, our momentum stolen in a single breath. Thank God there was nothing stored inside! A gap opened in the other side of the abandoned warehouse and we were drawn towards it.

I clung to Jamila like a drowning man to driftwood as the minibus finally rolled gently to a stop outside the warehouse's far wall. My ears were ringing. I heard the minibus door open. By the time I looked over, Driver Girl had gone, rocketing away from the vehicle at an Olympian pace. I couldn't blame her.

Jamila went limp as lettuce in my arms. 'Hey,' I breathed. 'It's OK. We're safe.'

Her eyes opened, big and dark. 'I tried to picture a hole in the wall . . . and it *happened*.'

'Yes, it did.' Feeling sick with a mixture of fear and relief, I helped her up from her seat and we staggered out of the minibus. 'Have to hand it to you, Jam. You weren't even properly awake and you saved us.'

'After I nearly killed us.' Jamila bit her lip, gazing at the hole in the side of the vehicle. 'In my mind I was throwing a hammer . . .'

'Straight into real life,' I agreed. 'Come on. The driver legged it and we should too.' I looked at the holes smashed in the sides of the abandoned warehouse.

'Someone's bound to turn up soon and ask a whole lot of questions that we don't want to answer . . .'

'You're right,' said Jamila, and pointed past me, up towards the sky.

A drone was hovering there, its camera lens trained on the two of us.

'Where did that thing come from?' I breathed. 'Someone's watching us!'

'Not for long,' said Jamila and with a swipe of her hand, the drone came apart in a shower of metal and plastic parts that peppered the concrete around us.

'Wow.' I looked at her warily. 'That took care of that. You OK?'

'Think there's any more of those drone things?' Jamila was looking about, haunted, sweat trickling down from her hairline. 'Whoever's watching could be just around the corner.'

'Let's go,' I suggested.

'I have to see.' Jamila pushed out her hands towards the warehouse . . . and the entire building toppled over like it was made of Duplo with the most deafening crash I'd ever heard. Bricks bounced everywhere in thick clouds of cement dust. I coughed, my hands clamped hard over my ears. Jamila puffed out a breath and the dust cleared in a handful of heartbeats. She stood, surveying the damage like a careless toddler who'd thrown her toys out of the pram.

I couldn't see any more drones and just then I didn't care. 'Right, we are leaving *now*.' I grabbed her by the arm and started to lead her away.

But then I found I couldn't move. My body was frozen still.

'Don't tell me what to do, Munday,' said Jamila quietly.

I couldn't move, not even my lips. Couldn't blink or swallow; it was like my whole body was holding its breath. I tried not to panic. The thump of my heart was still coming loud and I could feel the rush of blood in my temples as I fought against the paralysis. But what if all that stopped too?

Then suddenly I was falling forward, released. I fell to the ground and rolled over, staring up at Jamila, ready to shout my head off at her.

But she was gazing down at me, clearly terrified, tears streaming down her face. 'Oh, God, I'm so sorry. I didn't mean to, Danny. It's like I couldn't control myself . . .'

'But you can control everything else,' I said hoarsely. 'And that's a bad mix. Every cop in the city's gonna be out for this. Can we get away right now, please? Seriously. You need to rest.'

'Yeah. OK,' Jamila said. 'I think there's a bus stop at the top of the street . . .' She turned and stalked away from the disaster zone. I got up and followed, afraid she might turn her power on me again.

It was just an accident, I told myself. *I made plenty of mistakes when Adi gave me energenes.*

But that was exactly it – my powers had come from Adi. She was alien but she used her powers to help and protect, and so did I. Jamila's powers had come from Swarm agents – alien soldiers from the Hive Mind who wanted to remove human life.

If Jamila's mind had been affected by the Swarm's

bodyprinter . . . What the hell was I supposed to do?

Oh, Adi, I thought miserably. *I could really do with you here right now.*

But Adi had gone back into space, summoned by the Swarm; she'd developed an independent streak they didn't like and wound up paying the price. But how heavy was it?

I'd wondered what might have happened to her a thousand times, and never harder than right there and then at the bus stop back on the main road. Jamila had fallen asleep with her head on my shoulder, and I covered my face as a trail of speeding police cars howled past and swerved on to the potholed tarmac of the industrial estate. They would find a building that had fallen over by itself beside an abandoned minibus. I knew it wouldn't take long to follow the trail back to Mr Sunaki and my school who would want to know what the hell had gone down.

The bus finally came. I helped sleepy Jamila on board. We got a spot on the back seat. And as the bus pulled away slowly into the traffic, the bus stand's digital billboard caught my eye.

It was an ad for face cream or something. But the supermodel's face was flickering. My heart beat out a rising rhythm as I saw a different face trying to take its place: young, symmetrical. Highly cheekboned. Bright brown eyes, wide and pleading, banded with glitches and static.

I opened my mouth to shout: *Stop the bus! I need to go back . . . need to talk with her. She's the one person who could help . . . !*

But the face had already vanished from the billboard.

'No!' I banged my fist against the seat as I slumped back down beside Jamila.

'What is it?' Jamila murmured sleepily.

I didn't answer. Let it go. Chewed my lip.

But I was certain. Flickering there in the digital ad, I'd seen Adi's face.

CHAPTER THREE
IMPOSSIBLE SIGNALS

I got Jamila home in the end; she was burning with a fever, hardly able to walk by herself. Her mum threw her arms round her, took her off to bed, ready to feed her tasty family recipes that, she assured me, could see off any sickness you could name.

Confidence is good, I thought miserably, *but there's no name for what's wrong with Jamila.* I crossed to my home next door. Mum was still at work and the house stood as quiet and empty as the evening ahead with no Jam in it. I wondered how long it would take for the police to come knocking on the door. That minibus driver must have sprinted to the police and told them who'd she'd been carrying. With Jamila really poorly, she'd probably escape questioning for now – which meant that getting our story straight was down to me.

It's all right, I told myself. No one would believe a couple of kids would have anything to do with a hole in a minibus and a warehouse falling over.

But that camera drone had been watching. Whoever controlled it would know the truth.

Where were they now? Still watching?

And had I really seen Adi's face, or just imagined it?

Closing the curtains, I sat down in the middle of the living room in the gloom and hugged my knees and kept wishing my mum would get back from work.

A couple of hours later the universe finally listened. I almost jumped a mile when the front door rattled and Mum burst into the hallway. 'Danny?' she yelled. 'Where are you? What a day. What a day! Danny?'

Oh God, the police went straight to her! I thought. 'Uh . . .' I got up and opened the living room door. 'Everything all right?'

'You won't believe what happened!' Mum's blonde hair was as wild as the look in her eyes as she swept into the kitchen and tossed her empty travel cup into the sink. 'Jodrell Bank is on fire!'

'What?' I spluttered.

'Not literally,' Mum said quickly. 'I mean it's ablaze with scientific interest.' She opened the fridge and surveyed the unimpressive insides. 'Hmm. Did we eat the leftovers from that Chinese takeaway?'

'No. That was weeks ago,' I said patiently. 'It's probably evolved into a higher life form by now, opened the fridge door and moved out.'

She turned and looked at me. 'Then maybe that's the source of the readings we're picking up.'

I frowned. 'Huh?'

'Fast radio bursts, Danny!' Mum came over to me with a big grin on her face. 'We've picked up some unique FRBs!'

My stomach did a flip. I knew two hard facts about FRBs: one, they were weird little blasts of repeating radio waves zooming at the speed of light from distant galaxies and, two, the Swarm used them in secret to travel through outer space.

That must *have been Adi I saw*! I thought. And I suddenly wished that Adi hadn't used her alien powers to wipe Mum's memories of the Swarm. It meant I couldn't tell her my fears for Jamila, couldn't ask for her help or protection against whoever had sent that drone after me and Jam . . .

Whoever or *what*ever.

I pretended to yawn like I wasn't that bothered. 'Where did these fast radio thingies come from, then?'

'Well, that's why we're all fired up!' Mum lit the gas hob as if to prove it and plonked a pan of water on top of it. 'The FRBs came from close by. I don't mean like those signals we detected six years ago using the European Very Long Baseline Interferometry Network – you know, the ones that came from Messier 81.' She looked into the distance as if reliving a glorious memory. 'Ahh. Remember that day?'

'I was eight or something, Mum.'

'It was incredible. Amazing! That signal came from a galaxy twelve million light years away and it was *still* forty times closer than any other FRB, ever.' Mum poured some dried fusilli into the pan, scattering several of the yellow spirals over the countertop. 'Guess where today's

FRBs came from? You'll never guess. Never.' She picked up one of the dried pasta pieces and crunched on it, slowly at first but with increasing enthusiasm. 'Go on. Guess! You'll never guess, Danny.'

I shrugged. 'The edge of the solar system?'

'Ha! Wrong!' Mum grinned. 'Don't feel bad. No one in their right mind would guess it right. It's impossible. Almost certainly a glitch in the systems.' She held out another piece of pasta to me. 'Want one?'

'No.' I gritted my teeth. 'So where did the FRBs come from?'

'Right here on Earth,' Mum said. 'It couldn't have been the Chinese takeaway otherwise, could it? Duh! And Jodrell's the only place that picked it up, thanks to reflected signals from several low-orbit communication satellites as they travelled over the UK.'

Dutiful son, I tried to wrap my head round that. 'You mean . . . the FRBs were zapped from here into space but some of them bounced off the satellites?'

'Goofy, isn't it?' Mum seemed suddenly deflated. 'I mean, it's *got* to be false data – right? We were stupid to get all fired up.' She chomped morosely on a second dried fusillo. 'But what's life if you don't let yourself get excited now and then . . .'

'Mum,' I said, 'what time did you detect this signal?'

'This afternoon,' she said. 'That's why I'm late home again – sorry, Danny. Pasta's all right, isn't it? There's no sauce but I think we have some ketchup . . .'

'What time *exactly*,' I pressed her.

'Just after 5 p.m.,' Mum said, 'if you must know.'

I knew it. I remembered the news on the minibus radio saying it was five – just before Jamila's energenes blew the hell out of our transport, dismantled the drone and knocked over the warehouse.

Which meant that Jamila had to be the source of the FRBs. Most likely she'd made Adi's face appear on the bus-stop billboard, too.

'What're you going to do about these FRBs then?' I asked. 'I mean, probably nothing, right?'

'Absolutely everything, you mean!' Mum poured salt into the pan as the water started to boil. 'The night crew are checking the data from the satellites. Triangulating their positions over the country, we should be able to pinpoint where the impossible FRBs came from and scan for any more of them.'

Just point your scope at Jamila's bedroom next door, I thought, closing my eyes wearily.

Mum noticed. 'Hey, Danny, it's OK. There's bound to be a perfectly normal explanation. Don't be scared.'

But I was. Cos between drones and Jodrell Bank, it felt like danger was closing in for Jamila.

I went to bed early, head spinning with the unwelcome events of the day and stomach turning with pasta and ketchup. I knocked on Jamila's wall, hoping she might still be awake. We often knocked coded messages to each other through the brickwork.

Not tonight, though. There was no reply.

I turned off my bedside light at quarter to ten and hoped that sleep would drive the anxieties from my head.

I woke at 2 a.m. to find someone had turned on my TV. The flickering screen sent ghostly static dancing over the walls.

And suddenly Adi's face was staring out at me in bleary black and white.

In a heartbeat I was sitting bolt upright. 'Adi!' I breathed. 'Is that you?'

'Yes, Danny.' Adi's lips moved, out of synch with the words she formed. Her voice was faint and glitching. 'Listen,' she said. 'Danger. Danger is coming.'

'Danger for me?' I said. 'Danger for Jamila?'

'For you both,' Adi agreed. 'For Earth. For everyone.'

CHAPTER FOUR
GHOST

For a few seconds I clung to the hope that I was dreaming. But I knew I could never feel so cold inside from a dream. 'What kind of danger, Adi?' I whispered. 'What's going on? When did you get back to Earth?'

'This version of me never *left* the Earth,' Adi said, her digital image distorting with static. 'I am a shadow of myself. A prisoner.'

I shook my head. 'I don't understand you.'

'Listen.' Adi's eyes suddenly filled the screen. 'Do you remember the warehouse where I kept my digiscanner?'

I shivered. Just hearing her say the word made my insides shrink. Adi's kind, the Swarm, used a digiscanner to turn our living, breathing bodies into digital data – and a bodyprinter to make us flesh and blood again. I'd spent over three weeks as a digiscan, nothing more than a compressed speck of information travelling at light speed around the solar system. The memories of that time – and the way I came back to life in a brand-new body that was *made*, not born – still gave me nightmares.

Adi's image shimmered. 'When we came back there you could not find your phone. Do you remember?'

'Uh-huh.' How could I forget? Mum had taken weeks to replace my Samsung. 'I thought the Swarm agents took it, or it fell out my pocket someplace . . .'

'You lost it in that warehouse,' Adi told me. 'Some time ago, dangerous people found it. They discovered traces of me . . . my code . . . inside the phone's operating system.'

'Like a backup, you mean?' I said. 'A backup version of you?'

'Even deleted data can be recovered . . . if you have the talent and tools.' Adi's skin buzzed with static and her voice was like a tinny breath. 'They couldn't restore all of me . . . But they scraped out enough to make . . . the *ghost* of me.'

My head was buzzing like Spider-Man's when a

supervillain is close. Adi had made first contact with me through that phone. Like I said before, her digital form could travel through gadgets on the Wi-Fi. This image on the TV screen, it looked like Adi but it wasn't real. Just like a digital photo of a sports car wasn't an actual sports car.

'The ghost of you.' I got out of bed and crossed to the screen. 'You're not . . . in pain are you?'

'Pain is an emotional response, Danny, transmitted through sensory nerve fibres only in biological—'

'OK, OK, I get it. So what is . . . wrong with you?'

'I am incomplete. Powerless,' Ghost Adi whispered. 'And you are in danger. Whoever found the phone knows it is yours. They have been watching you and Jamila. I have seen the video taken by their drones. It is stored in the same hard drive that contains me.'

I felt a deeper chill. 'That explains what it was doing at the industrial park. It must have trailed us from the playing fields. So they were watching when Jamila let rip with her powers?'

'Yes. I tried to reach you . . . to warn you . . .'

'At the bus stop, you mean?'

'To warn you . . .' Adi blipped out completely, then reappeared, fainter than before. A proper ghost. 'They know now . . . about Jamila's energenes.'

'Who knows?' I said. 'And what do they want?'

Ghost Adi shifted in a scatter of pixels. 'What else? With the power of energenes they could make the ultimate weapon.'

'They could,' I agreed. 'Whoever *they* are.' With energenes you could twist the physical world around your fingers – not so much point-and-click but point-and-*think*. 'What are they gonna do, then? Try to kidnap her or something?'

Ghost Adi nodded: 'They *will* take her. And attempts to harvest the energenes will damage Jamila beyond repair.'

'*Kill* her, you mean?' My heart was pulling wheelies behind my ribs. 'No. No, no, no. Can't happen. No way. What are we going to do?'

'This time, there is no "we",' Ghost Adi said sadly. 'I am a prisoner.'

'But you're here,' I argued. 'In my TV.'

'Only an echo of me. And even that will be missed if I do not return to my prison.'

'Where are you being held?' I asked her.

'I cannot tell. It's being hidden from me.'

'Adi, come on! You must be able to do *something!*' I caught myself almost shouting and put my hands over my mouth, worried that Mum might come barging in. But there was no tell-tale creak from the landing; the house was dead quiet. 'Please, Adi. Don't go. Help me think of something.' I rapped my knuckles against the wall. 'Jamila's behind there and she's in danger.'

'Danger. Yes. Not only from the watchers,' said Ghost Adi gravely. 'The energenes now activating inside Jamila came from a bodyprinter designed for Swarm agents – that's true, isn't it?'

'Yes,' I agreed, and realised that if she had to ask, Adi really must be incomplete.

'These energenes are changing Jamila . . . too powerful for her mind or body to control.'

I remembered the way Jam had stopped me from moving – *'Don't tell me what to do, Munday'* – and felt dread like cold water filling my stomach. 'There's only one way to save her then,' I said. 'Digiscan her body and print it out again – *without* energenes.'

'But I can't build a working digiscanner, Danny. Not any more.' The image on the screen was barely visible through the darkness. 'I am only an echo of myself. That knowledge is lost to me . . . and I have no way to assemble the technology required. If only you could do something . . .'

'I wish!' I wanted to cry. 'This is our fault. Jamila only turned herself digital in the first place for our sake, remember? She saved us . . .'

Saved.

'Oh, wait. *Wait.* Hang on a second.' I remembered Jamila telling me how she'd done it: '*I just stuck my SIM card into the bodyprinter . . . Adi had done something to it. It sorted everything for me.*'

And I still had the SIM card.

I turned and rushed to my bedside table and yanked open the drawer. 'Oh, let me still be able to find it . . . Yes!'

'Danny?' the ghost of Adi whispered. '*What* have you found?'

'The tech you put on to this SIM let Jamila turn a bodyprinter into a digiscanner!' I proudly held up the little card. 'If I can get the data on here to you, maybe you'll figure out how to save Jamila?'

'Oh, *yes*, Danny! If you can get some of the parts I will need . . .' Adi's ghost glowed stronger, candle bright on the screen. 'Quickly. Put the SIM card in your phone. I can absorb the data it contains through your Wi-Fi . . .'

'You can?' I hardly dared believe it. 'But I thought you were trapped.'

'There will be more traces of my code in the SIM. It will make me stronger.'

'It had better,' I muttered, already jabbing the end of a twisted paper clip into the tiny hole in my phone that opened the SIM card tray.

'Munday?' came a muffled voice through the wall.

'Jamila,' I whispered, taking out my old SIM.

'Quickly, Danny,' Ghost Adi urged me. 'I need that data. I sense danger.'

'Munday,' Jamila was shouting now. 'What are you doing?'

'Shush!' I slotted in the SIM and restarted the phone as I ran to the wall. 'Jamila, stay quiet.'

'She's here, isn't she? Adi!' Jamila suddenly appeared – straight through the wall. Shaking and sweating, she turned to the TV. 'Adi, you did this to me. You made me a freak. You're killing me!'

'It's not me!' The picture of Ghost Adi suddenly flared, then came back sharper. 'Jamila, you must get out of here, quickly. Danny—'

The image froze on the screen, like the TV had crashed. Then the glass cracked and the screen went dead. I stared in horror as my TV folded in on itself like a ball of paper crumpled in the hand of a child. Jamila was holding out her fists.

'Jam, no!' I took hold of her shoulders and stared into her glassy eyes, trying to connect. 'Listen, you're not well. You have to rest . . .'

She broke free of my grip. Then, like something out of a scary movie, she floated backwards away from me. A split in the wall opened like a mouth to swallow her.

Barely a minute later there was a thump and a crash and I heard Jam's mum scream wildly from the other side of the wall.

I heard someone run inside: Jam's dad. 'What happened?' He sounded as terrified as I felt.

'Call the ambulance,' her mum wailed. 'Jamila's hardly breathing. I think she's dying!'

CHAPTER FIVE
HOSPITAL TRIP

Not even Mum could sleep through all of that, and she was already up with me in her dressing gown when Jamila's dad banged on our door a few minutes later. He looked drawn and anxious.

'We're taking Jim-Jam to hospital, Lydia,' he told Mum. 'I'm so sorry to ask, but can you keep an eye on Farid and Daria? They're shaken up, shouldn't be alone right now.'

'Of course,' she said. 'What's wrong with Jamila?'

Mr al-Sufi was already running down the path to the family car. 'We don't know.'

Lucky you, I thought morosely as he got in the passenger side and Jamila's mum stamped on the gas. I glimpsed Jamila bundled up in a blanket in the backseat as the car pulled away.

'I'm sure she'll be all right,' Mum told me. 'I'd better pop across.'

'Yeah. Right,' I said and closed the door heavily behind her. The one scrap of comfort I could find was that Jamila would be surrounded by doctors and nurses and porters as well as her parents. Any creepy kidnappers out there would find it hard to get to her.

But could the hospital do anything else to help?

I thought of my crushed TV upstairs and a heavy wave of tiredness crashed over me. One more impossible thing to explain. I felt a stab of resentment for the Swarm and all the weird, mind-bending stuff they'd brought into my life. All these past months I'd been thinking about Adi, missing her, wondering where she might be. Now I'd seen her – or something like her – I only felt more miserable.

I went back to my bedroom and as I got inside, my phone buzzed.

It was a message sent from a string of numbers I didn't recognise, way too long to be a proper contact.

Good your mum out next door, it read. *We can*

go to hospital.

I frowned and texted back, *Adi?*

Borrow parts for bodyprinter from medical equipment, she wrote back.

'We can't do that,' I said out loud. 'Patients really need that equipment.' I began to type back but there was no need; Adi was listening in through the phone.

Save Jamila, she typed.

'When you put it that way,' I muttered.

The phone buzzed yet again. *Get dressed,* came the message. *I've called a taxi.*

'Bossy, much?' I muttered. But there was no reply and I did as she'd said. It stood to reason there would be parts for a bodyprinter at the hospital. The machine Adi built in the old warehouse looked like Frankenstein's spray-tan booth with all sorts of machines bolted on. One of them looked like an MRI scanner; you know, like a large tube with a table in the middle and you have to stay dead still while they fire magnetic fields and radio waves to create an image of your insides. Yep, radio waves. That would fit well with the Swarm way of doing stuff.

I watched out for the taxi, praying that Mum wouldn't hear it pull up from next door and go to see and then spot me leaving the house. When it finally came, it was one of those driverless cabs.

'I'm not getting in one of those!' I said flatly.

It has passed the necessary technical checks and safety laws. Adi messaged. *Have you never been in one before?*

'Yes, with you!' I retorted. 'You tricked me into getting into one. Don't you remember?'

There was a long pause. Then finally the inevitable buzz.

No.

I got into the taxi. Me, Adi and Jamila: what had happened to us! The last time we'd been together I'd felt supercharged for the win, the three of us running riot over impossible odds. Now things had kicked off again but we were weak, sick or broken, stumbling about in the dark with no plan, no promise and precious little hope.

The pre-paid taxi took us to the drop off area outside the hospital and I got out feeling anxious. 'Where now?'

Radiology, Adi texted.

'Can we just check how Jamila is doing?' I asked.

The buzz again: *Radiology*.

I knew I had to take no for an answer. Jam's parents were with her and if they saw me they'd tell my mum and, boom, so much for a secret mission stealing high tech stuff from a hospital. And while the thought of doing that made me feel sick, the thought of Jamila in so much pain and danger made me feel sicker. Only I knew what was really wrong with her, and only I could help put things right. This version of Adi might be a shadow of her proper self but if she could just outwit the creepy creeps keeping her down . . . She'd come off best before, and against worse. And she'd always watched out for me and Jam.

I felt embers of positivity stir inside. We could turn this round. I knew it.

Now, where the hell was the radiology department? I found a sign that told me to follow green lines on the floor, so I did, wondering what I'd say if anyone challenged me. It was quieter in this part of the hospital. I guess at 3 a.m. people aren't queuing up to use the MRI unless there is an emergency.

Well, for sure, Jamila was an emergency.

Lights flickered on, triggered by my presence as I reached radiology. I saw CCTV cameras in the ceiling. Heart skipping, I half-expected squads of security guards to pile in on me. The whole place was empty: no one waiting, no staff on duty. The only noise was a clang and clatter from somewhere up ahead.

Turn left into the corridor, Adi texted to my phone. *Room B34*

I tucked the phone in my pocket and followed the directions. They took me closer to the banging sounds. Maintenance team, I supposed. With non-stop patients during the day, they'd have to do their work at night when it was quiet.

There were doors all along the corridor, helpfully labelled. B19 . . . B22 . . . I paused beside a snack machine in an alcove and my eyes lingered until I saw the little digital displays showing the prices. Three quid for a tiny carton of juice! No thanks.

The clash and batter of the maintenance team was getting louder. Only it sounded more like they were demolishing something than keeping it in working order. Still, the racket might be a useful cover if me and Adi would be removing parts from an MRI scanner.

Room B34 was one door down and marked observation. Hoping no one had observed my coming here, I glanced about the empty corridor before I went inside.

And with a chill I saw the snack machine was no longer displaying its prices. The cold green little digits had changed to show something even more frightening.

Now every single one read:

RUN DANNY.

But of course, I didn't run. My tired brain jolted with the shock and I hesitated. I knew that only Adi could send a message like that, and she was already texting me through my phone. Unless— Jamila . . . ?

I only thought it over for a couple of seconds, tops.

But by then I realised the banging noise had stopped.

As I was about to bolt, a man's hand shot straight through the closed wooden door in front of me. His fingers closed on my T-shirt and he hauled me into room B34.

Somehow I passed straight through the wood without it breaking, in a blur of movement. I was in a soft-lit room with a glass partition wall. Through it I could see the MRI scanner lying in pieces. Torn apart.

Too stunned to freak out, I realised the man who'd pulled me through was still holding on to me. He was big – over two metres tall with powerful muscles barely contained by a black jumpsuit. His dark hair was pulled back in a ponytail and his eyes were icy blue and narrowed.

I struggled in his grip, but the man lifted me into the air like I weighed nothing and tossed me against the wall. I fell sprawling to the floor with a cry, bruising my elbow. The man loomed over me and a meaty hand closed around my windpipe.

I choked, gripped his wrist with both hands to try and break his grip, but I might as well have been a baby struggling with an elephant's trunk. He lifted me to my feet and slammed me back against the wall again.

'Careful, Beta,' a woman said, nearby. 'He has something we need, remember?' The voice was familiar but I couldn't place it, and I couldn't see past 'Beta', whose bulk filled my vision. For all his strength, though, there was a smell of sickness about him. He was unnaturally pale, with dark veins criss-crossing his skin like a map of the London Underground.

'Who are you?' I asked, fighting to keep the shake from my words.

A woman with dyed red hair, dressed in a long white doctor's coat, pushed past him. 'Surprise, Danny,' she said, and when she smiled she showed a set of train-track-type braces. And suddenly I knew just where I'd seen her before.

'The driver,' I whispered hoarsely. 'The minibus that collected Jamila and me . . . you drove it.'

'And your friend broke it,' the woman agreed. 'Don't worry, Danny. We'll make sure that Jam keeps things under control from now on.' She looked at Beta. 'Under our control.'

Beta smiled at this. His teeth were grey, unexpectedly small and neat and, like the woman's, were fixed with that unusual design of metal braces. 'The phone's in his jacket,' he said with a breath of Eastern Europe about his accent.

'Thank you,' the woman said. She reached into my pocket and daintily plucked out the phone.

'You can't have that,' I hissed.

'Don't fret, Danny. I only want the SIM.' She pulled a little metal pin from her lapel and worked it into the hole in the side of the phone to eject the SIM tray.

'No, don't!' I pleaded. Adi was in that SIM card and so were the plans for the digiscanner. That had to be why the MRI was already in pieces; this weird couple had known what to take. I lunged forward and tried to snatch it back – but Beta hurled me into the observation window. I banged my head on the glass and it was like the world exploded into red sparks. *How did this guy get so strong?* I thought dimly. Was it my imagination or were there little sparks dancing around his teeth? I couldn't really tell. I was losing consciousness.

'Leave Jamila alone,' I remember saying.

'Leave her?' the woman said softly. 'We're just getting started.'

I woke up with a jolt, just where I'd been left – in a heap

on the hospital floor. I got up, aching all over, and the dreadful memories came whooshing back. *Jamila*, I thought. *I've got to check she's OK. Doesn't matter if Jam's parents see me here. Got to find her.*

Before someone found *me*, trespassing next to an MRI scanner that had been stripped down for parts.

I picked up my discarded phone but my heart felt left flat on the ground. With no SIM I couldn't receive any more Adi texts – and somehow our message stream had been wiped clean. Leaving the room, I saw the snack-machine display was normal again.

All alone and tired, I decided to head for the casualty department to track Jamila down. As I walked, my throbbing head felt thick with questions. How had the driver woman known about my SIM in the first place – and where had she and her pet man-mountain come from? Big Bad Beta had been packing energenes for sure. Could he be a Swarm agent? There was something that felt not quite human about him. But why would the Swarm have come back to Earth again? The real Adi was back with them already and they'd know how to build bodyprinters, digiscanners and anything else. So why take the SIM?

The questions chased their tails through the queasy corners of my mind. Despite everything, though, I was so relieved when I reached A&E with nothing bad happening. I queued at the counter and finally got to speak with the frazzled-looking woman at reception.

'Can you tell me where I can find Jamila al-Sufi, please?' I asked.

'Al-Sufi?' She frowned and checked her computer. 'Don't think we've had anyone of that name in this evening.'

'You have,' I said automatically.

She blinked, cold and disapproving. 'There's no one of that name listed here.'

'But her parents brought her in!' I protested.

Literally, just as I spoke their name, they appeared. They looked dazed but calm as they stepped out of a corridor into the main reception.

'Never mind, *they*'ll tell me where Jamila is,' I said. 'Mr al-Sufi! Mrs al-Sufi, is everything OK with Jamila?'

'Danny!' said Jam's mum. 'Hello, love, everything all right? What are you doing in the hospital?'

'I'm here cos of Jamila, of course,' I said. 'You're not just leaving her here by herself, are you?'

'Leave who here?' Mr al-Sufi looked baffled. 'What's going on, Danny? Where's your mum?'

'You should know, you asked her to babysit,' I reminded him, 'while you took Jamila here.'

'Jamila?' Mrs al-Sufi looked completely lost.

'Yes! Jamila. Jim-Jam.' I felt a chill snake its way down my backbone. 'Your daughter.'

'What are you talking about?' Mrs al-Sufi stared at me. 'We don't have a daughter named Jamila.'

CHAPTER SIX
MISSING, BELIEVED NON-EXISTENT

Of all the impossible stuff I'd experienced, I never thought the hardest to believe would be my own ears. But there was no arguing; Mr and Mrs al-Sufi swore blind that they only had a boy called Farid and a girl called Daria at home.

'Then why are you here now?' I demanded.

They swapped looks. 'It's a family matter,' said Mr al-Sufi.

'Yes, that's right. A family matter,' Mrs al-Sufi agreed.

More like, the Brace Twins got to you, I thought miserably.

'Come along now, Danny,' said Mrs al-Sufi, more softly. 'Would you like a ride home with us?'

The night was still big and dark outside, and I was shaky on my legs. 'That would be great, Mrs al-Sufi,' I said, while actually thinking, *You're gonna get the world's biggest shock when you find one of your bedrooms belongs to a daughter you never heard of . . .*

I was fidgeting all the way home in the back of the car. I almost herded the al-Sufis along their drive like chickens, I was so keen for them to see the evidence with their own eyes.

As they neared the door Mum opened it with a smile. 'Hope you took care of that family matter?' she said. 'Hello, Danny, why are you here?'

'Just checking on Jamila,' I said.

'Who?' said Mum.

As was fast becoming my basic state, I felt sick. 'I, uh, left something in her room . . .' Pushing past Mum, I ran upstairs.

'Danny!' Mr al-Sufi barked. 'What are you doing?'

'Wait till you see this,' I muttered, flinging open Jam's bedroom door.

It was empty.

Usually it looked like a bomb site. Now all her stuff was gone: her bed, all the posters, her Moon lamp, the shelves shaped like a fire escape, the soft toys she kept saying she was going to bin but never did. Everything had vanished. The Brace Twins must have got in here, taken stuff. Or just blitzed the room with energenes. Even the carpet held no mark of the furniture that had stood here.

Mum came up behind me. 'Danny, I don't know what's so fascinating in the al-Sufis' spare room, but you're showing me up. It's late – can we go home now, please?'

I wanted to turn and shout at her, *Jamila is real! Your minds have been messed with, can't you see – no one is acting normal!* But I couldn't look at anyone because I didn't want them to see the tears creeping into my eyes.

Home we went, me and Mum, with Jamila's parents glaring at me like I was evil to the core. Mum didn't say anything besides a cheery 'Goodnight!' as she went off to her room, as if nothing had happened. I didn't answer. I was checking my contacts on my phone.

Jamila had been deleted. So had the pictures of me and her – anything that showed her face at least. *It's like she's been wiped from existence*, I thought. *Like a computer virus eating through reality, deleting all trace of her.* In

might've been a villain's henchman in a Marvel movie. I couldn't see the police exactly jumping on the information.

So I just cycled around each evening looking for them myself, feeling more and more helpless. I was so used to sharing everything with Jamila, and now she wasn't there. She never *had* been there as far as everyone else was concerned.

Still, I clung to the hope she could still be alive. Maybe bad people were running tests and experiments on her, but they couldn't be through with her yet. They'd gone to tons of effort wiping Jamila from the minds of everyone who knew her so no one would come looking. Maybe it would take them months to do all that they wanted to.

And whenever I thought of her, my brain burned with the need to do something, anything. Sometimes – the darkest, most sleepless times – I half wished I could've forgotten her too. Why hadn't I? I could only think it was down to Adi somehow. I'd come out of her bodyprinter; maybe that had done something to my mind?

I wished so hard I had some way to find Jamila.

Then it zapped me like lightning.

The FRBs that Mum had been on about that day; the radio bursts that the satellites had picked up. The team at Jodrell Bank were going to use them to work out the source of the signals . . . and I happened to know the source – or one of the sources, at least – was Jamila. The Swarm might have been able to wipe the thought of Jamila from people's minds, but they couldn't wipe her powers. They wanted them. Needed them.

Driver's smile in the hospital bit hard into my memory. *'We're just getting started.'*

Wouldn't that mean more bursts coming through?

I cycled back home at breakneck speed. Unbelievably, Mum was actually around. She was perched on a stool in the kitchen beside enough empty coffee cups to form a herd. Her top was devoid of stains, smears and crumbs, which felt serious; clearly Mum had not been eating.

'I didn't go into work today,' she admitted. 'Migraine. My head feels like someone's been slamming doors in it.'

Because they kind-of have, I thought. 'That's rough,' I said, cos compassion should always come before a big ask, right? 'So, anyway. Did your mates at work manage to track down the source of those super-fast radio waves from the Earth?'

Mum winced and I wondered if I'd spoken too loud. 'Yeah, the first ones looked to be coming not far from here actually. Since then we've detected more bursts, in the south of England, outside London. But it's been checked out and the place is clean.'

They've detected more! I thought, trying to hide my excitement. *Jamila's energenes, they've got to be.*

'Most likely explanation is there are faulty receptors on the telescope array,' Mum went on.

I knew better but I just nodded. 'What was this place outside London, then?'

'Only a boring old manor house.' Mum stood up from her stool and stretched. 'Like I say, they've checked the building and the grounds but there's no sign of anything unusual.'

'Who's *they*?'

'The British Special Cybersecurity Unit.' Mum put on a haughty voice. 'We were notified by the director herself.'

'Araminta Pearce?' I blurted out.

'*Doctor* Pearce, yes.' Mum frowned. 'How'd you know about her?'

Because Pearce ended up falling under the Swarm's control and helped them try to catch and kill me, was the honest answer. But I didn't think that would go down so well. 'Oh, I, uh, think I saw the name on your laptop one time.'

'Oi. Don't snoop, Danny. That information is highly sensitive.' Mum sighed. 'And so's my head. Excuse me while I snoop for paracetamol.'

Mum shuffled out. She wasn't even out the door before I had flipped open her laptop and typed in her password. Or rather, her passnumber: my birthday (aww) followed by the date of her divorce from Dad (less aww). Her email was open. I saw one headed 'NO GO ON FRB SOURCE' and clicked on it. Skimming it, I saw apologies, complaints and coordinates, so I took a quick picture on my phone before closing the mail and the laptop in short order. Just as Mum came back in.

'By the way,' I said smoothly, taking inspiration from

her passnumber. 'Dad's back from Hawaii – he's in the country, did you know?'

'No.' Mum frowned. 'Hmm. Maybe that's the reason I've got this migraine.'

'He's got a science conference in London,' I went on. 'He's asked me to come down and meet him. Tomorrow.'

'Tomorrow? By yourself?'

'It's, like, two-and-a-half hours,' I said. 'I'm not a little kid. And it's a Saturday. Loads of kids on the train.'

'Dad didn't say anything to me about coming over. I thought we'd been getting on better, too.' She looked sad, and I felt awful. 'Well. Has he bought you a ticket?'

'Uh, yeah. And Dad said he'll meet me halfway, in Coventry.' Even I was surprised at the quality of the lies spilling from my lips. I felt bad conning Mum – especially about Dad – but reminded myself that I was doing it for Jamila. For my best mate who the whole world had forgotten about. Going through official channels wasn't an option.

'All right, then. You've got money in your account and my bank card details on your phone too, haven't you?

In case you need anything?'

Like a train ticket and a taxi fare to wherever those coordinates show, I thought. 'Yep. It's on there.'

'Just promise you'll sit next to the emergency pull cord if you can and sit with nice people.'

'I'll give them a "Nice Questionnaire" to fill in before I agree to park my bum anywhere near them,' I told her.

'Glad to hear.' Mum winced and rubbed her head. 'I think I might go to bed, love.'

'I won't be late either,' I said. 'Night!'

Tomorrow was a big day. I would get train tickets, travel into London and somehow find my way to the location from there. Maybe I'd find something that Pearce and her cybersecurity squad had missed.

I didn't know if Jamila would still be there. It might've been Beta's energenes that Jodrell Bank had detected, not Jam's at all.

But I had to find out.

CHAPTER SEVEN
TRAIN TRAP

Have you ever been on a train journey, looking out the window, and then you notice your reflection? Your face and head, transparent, as the world rushes by straight through it. Like you're a ghost.

I had that feeling as I sat slumped in my seat, watching the grimy landscape through grimy glass. It was all so ordinary, and yet the reason for my being here was anything but. I felt conspicuous, like the secrets I held were shining out to everyone else in the carriage. *My friend can bend reality! She's been abducted by creatures from the Virgo Supercluster disguised as ordinary people!* And the worst secret of all: *I'm desperately trying to find her, cos . . .*

Cos Jamila's being this way is all my fault.

I didn't like to admit it even to myself. But if I'd never struck up a friendship with Adi . . . if I'd refused to help her and walked away . . . Well, then, I'd never have been taken into space to be held prisoner by an alien swarm. And Jamila would never have come after me. She'd have stayed herself – normal – not someone translated into ones and zeroes and then back again, with extra alien DNA spliced in along the way.

There again, if we hadn't helped Adi, the whole of humanity would have been wiped from the face of the planet. We'd all have wound up digital brains in an alien Swarm nation. But nobody knew that but me. No one would ever know what Jamila had sacrificed.

I really wished my lie was true and Dad *was* in the country. And as we stopped at Coventry, I really, really wished he was there to meet me like I'd pretended. I stared at my phone for the thousandth time, willing Adi to send me some sign that she was OK.

There was nothing. Only a weird tingle at the back of my neck, like the hairs there were standing up. I turned around but there was only a bunch of people pushing through the carriage in search of seats. A draught was blowing in through the open doors. It looked like rain.

With a sigh, I looked again at my stolen snapshot of the message on Mum's laptop. I'd pretty much memorised it, for all the use it was: '. . . extensive scan revealed no trace of scientific equipment, let alone the power requirements to generate such intense signals. Conclude FRBs could not originate here, source address incorrect.'

The incorrect address in question was in a village called Beckwith, a well-heeled town in Buckinghamshire, just outside Greater London. I would have to travel from Euston to Marylebone, get a train out to Beaconsfield Station and then a bus or a taxi to the house itself.

It might all be the wildest of wild goose chases. Then again, it might not. Because Dr Pearce and her team would have been searching for the obvious: superswishy tech, a big pile of incredible equipment that could throw out radio waves in megapowerful blasts. They didn't know that people could give off those same bursts of energy, given contact with the Swarm.

They had no idea how powerful such people were. But I did. The thought made me shiver again. What would I do if I got found out, or caught? No one would come looking. Nobody even knew where I was.

What the flip was I thinking? I was fourteen years old; suddenly I really felt it.

You can do this, I told myself. *When the Swarm kicked off, End of the World met Start of the Week, and Munday won.*

I decided to write everything down in a letter and send it to myself first class when I got off the train. It ought to arrive on Monday; if something happened and I wasn't able to get in touch with Mum, she'd know something bad had happened and would obviously read a letter addressed to her son in his own handwriting. I'd say just where I was going – even if not exactly why – and tell her to send the police there to raid the place. Or if they wouldn't listen, to put a rocket up Dr Araminta Pearce and tell her to check out the place properly this time . . .

I pulled out my hardcopies of the train schedules and a biro. On the back of one of the pages I started writing. It struck me: these could be my last ever written words. The thought freaked me out, and so I put off the writing by crafting myself a sort of envelope from the other sheet of paper. It wouldn't be much use at containing a letter though. I had no glue stick, no tape . . .

As if reading my mind, a woman behind me said, 'How are you going to hold it together?'

I turned in surprise. Saw dyed red hair. Teeth and braces bared in a train-tracked grin.

I was face to face with the SIM stealer. The driver. The woman who'd attacked me in the hospital.

I made to get up, but she put a hand on my shoulder and pushed me back into the seat with unnatural strength. No one else in the carriage seemed to notice. I gasped, then opened my mouth to shout for help.

But my throat closed before I could make a sound. Suddenly I couldn't breathe. I saw the woman's hand, like a slowly closing pincer. *She's choking me*, I realised. *Darth Vader style, without even touching me.* And still no one else was even glancing over. All rigidly looking down at their laps, as if in shame.

They were being controlled. No doubt this woman had energenes, just like her Beta buddy.

'I asked you how you were going to hold it together,'

she said. 'I wasn't talking about your little envelope.'

I did my best not to panic. To stay calm. This woman wasn't going to kill me. She could've done that already if she wanted. I raised my eyebrows, the only challenge I could make. She smiled and I saw that her braces had started to glow with a pale blue light – like they were drawing power or something. Finally she opened her hand and I fell back.

'Strong I am with the Force,' she said in a bad impression of Yoda. The glowing braces were fading back to plain metal. 'That is what you were thinking, isn't it, Danny? About *Star Wars*?'

She was right but I wasn't going to tell her that. 'I was thinking you've taken *Bluetooth* to a whole other level,' I said – not the greatest comeback, but I thought that any crack at all was impressive under the circumstances. 'How come you and Beta both wear those things. It's something to do with your powers, isn't it?'

'Don't concern yourself with such tiny details. There's so much more to worry about.'

Don't I know it. I wanted to shout for help, but what

could anyone do? I'd be risking their lives. Or their sanity. Besides, even if I got away this woman obviously had the power to find me.

'Who are you?' I asked.

'You can call me Zenia,' she said. 'Dr Zenia Biàn. And don't worry about your fellow passengers – I've suggested that they doze for a few minutes.'

Suggested. Right. 'So you hypnotise people and read their minds? You could work in a circus.'

'I'm actually a research scientist. A pioneer of digital biosynthesis.'

I blinked. 'Of *what* now?'

'Come on, Danny. Break it down, like Mr Fanning shows you in English.' Zenia smiled, well aware how creepy it was to be namedropping my teachers. 'Digital data is made up of a series of exact number values. That's how we can copy it, cut it, edit it so easily – we just duplicate the numbers.'

I couldn't believe this woman had hunted me down just to give me a lecture, but I played along. 'And bio is like . . . biology?'

'Bio means life. Organic life is not exact; it flows and it grows in unpredictable ways. Much harder to copy, or to make. And synthesis – well, that means *putting together*. Combining things to make something new.'

Obvs, I knew where this was going. 'You're putting together digital and organic life to make something new,' I said.

'And now you want to know where Jamila is, and if she's all right.' Zenia nodded. 'I don't need to be a mind reader to know that.'

'So just tell me,' I said.

'Of course.' She smiled again. 'Come and join my colleagues in first class. It's more private.'

'Uh, I don't know about that. My mum made me promise to sit with people who were nice.'

'If you care about your mother's safety, come and join us, Danny. Now.'

'What's the matter,' I said. 'Can't you keep all these people under control? Magic braces low on charge or something?'

Her smile stayed in place, only somehow her teeth

seemed less white than before. Greyer. 'You were coming to find us anyway. We're only saving you time and trouble.' Zenia glanced behind her. 'Of course, if you prefer Beta to carry you . . .'

My skin crawled as I saw the big guy who'd trounced me at the hospital squeeze through the sliding doors at the other end of the carriage. He stood staring across at me like a huge statue.

'OK. Fine.' I got up and shrugged. 'Take me to your leader.'

'Our *director*,' Zenia corrected me. 'She's waiting. And she's not at all happy that confidential information concerning fast radio bursts from the British Special Cybersecurity Unit has been accessed by a teenager.'

These people really did know everything I realised as Zenia shepherded me towards Beta – although he was so big, perhaps it was gravity dragging me towards him. He turned and lumbered along the gangway ahead of me and I followed.

But as Beta led the way into the first-class compartment, I realised that there really was no escaping the forces that held me. A woman sat working at the table. With a laptop, some papers, reading glasses on a chain around her neck and a cup of tea beside her, she looked like an ordinary businesswoman. And in her public life, she undoubtedly was.

See, I knew her. Her hair, the colour of ash. The drawn features, the cloud of quiet gloom about her. She looked up at me. 'Hello, Danny.'

Dread filled my stomach as things fell into place.

'Pearce,' I breathed. 'Dr Araminta Pearce.'

CHAPTER EIGHT
A DANGEROUS PLACE

'Sit down, Danny,' said Pearce. 'Would you like some tea?'

'No. I wouldn't.' I didn't sit down either. 'Well. This explains your Cybersecurity Unit drawing a blank on the house in Beaconsfield.'

'Obviously we're not keen to draw attention to our activities there.' Pearce's smile grew a notch tighter. 'Attention other than yours, Danny, at any rate. You can help us.'

'Help you?' I shrugged. 'Don't see how.'

'You can help in all sorts of ways,' said Zenia. 'With Jamila . . . and with Adi.'

I licked my dry lips. 'Who?'

'Don't insult our intelligence.' When I didn't follow up, Pearce tutted impatiently. 'Danny, I'm one of the few people on this planet who you can actually talk to truthfully about what you've been through. Don't squander the chance.'

'It sounds like between you, you know everything about everyone,' I said, slumping into the seat opposite Pearce. 'I just don't get *how* you know about Adi. She said she'd wiped the minds of everyone who'd seen or heard of her. Mum, you, everyone.'

'Except for you, Danny, and Jamila.' Pearce leaned back in her seat, scrutinising me. 'Perhaps because you've both come through a bodyprinter, Adi couldn't affect your minds in the same way?'

'Or perhaps because we're friends,' I said hotly. 'She didn't want us to forget her.'

Pearce's eyes had lit up and she nodded slowly. 'So. There really *is* a bond of friendship between you.'

Zenia nodded. 'With Adi being alien, so different from us, we assumed she'd simply exploited you to help in her ambitions.'

'You're right,' I said. 'She *is* different from you.' *Closer to being human for a start*, I thought privately. I hated that they'd already managed to extract information from me. I had to be more careful. *Ask* questions instead of answer them too freely. 'How come you can even remember her?'

'Adi was able to wipe people's minds but less tidy when it came to other evidence. Particularly the non-digital variety.' Zenia smiled. 'Like the visitors' book at Jodrell Bank reception. It showed that all sorts of outside contractors had visited to install and assemble advanced electronic components. No payments were made but it was as if some kind of superadvanced computer was being constructed on the premises.'

The quantum computer, I thought. The Swarm built one all right. Almost ended the human race with it. But I said nothing.

'Since there was no trace of any advanced electronics left on site, the bosses suspected our systems had been tampered with. As director, I looked into it.' Pearce shrugged. 'The only place I could think of where materials might have been stored was the old nuclear bunker. No one had set foot there for almost forty years. At least, that's what we thought. But when I looked I found evidence that showed *you* there. You and this Adi.'

'The security cameras in the bunker were installed in the 1980s,' Zenia put in. 'They're motion activated, record on to old VHS videotape. Videotape isn't digital tech, of course . . .'

'So it didn't show on Adi's radar,' I realised. 'She didn't think to wipe it.'

'Watching the tapes, seeing you both . . . it triggered the memories Adi had tried to wipe,' Pearce said. 'I remembered coming to your house with the Unit to capture you . . . threatening your mother . . . Confronting you both in the warehouse by the river . . .'

'And you went back to the warehouse, didn't you,' I supposed, remembering what Ghost Adi had told me over my TV set. 'You found my old phone – scraped the traces of Adi out of it.'

Pearce nodded. 'And I realised what advances Swarm technology could bring to humanity.'

'I agreed,' Zenia murmured and looked over at the impassive Beta. 'What an incredible opportunity . . . to synthesise human and digital beings in one life form.'

'Using energenes,' I realised. 'Only you don't know it all, do you? Or you wouldn't need Jamila. You wouldn't need me. You tried to rebuild Adi but you couldn't do it, could you?'

'Tried?' Pearce's tight smile grew more smug. 'We could have recreated Adi exactly.'

'Or rather, *Adi* could've,' Zenia said softly.

'Adi's code is programmed to repair itself,' Pearce went on, 'and it started to do so at an incredible rate. If she became whole, she would be too powerful to control. To contain her long enough to extract knowledge and skills – such as the secret of creating energenes for our own use – from her, we had to . . . limit her powers.'

'You crippled her,' I hissed. 'She's just a ghost of herself . . .'

Zenia raised an eyebrow. 'How would you know about poor little Ghost Adi, Danny?'

Once again, I was reminded of what a lousy spy I'd make. But I figured it was my only hope to rattle them; make them think twice about what they were doing. 'You think you've got Adi under lock and key? Well, you don't.'

Pearce frowned. 'Don't we?'

'Adi got out. Came to me. Warned me what you were planning. We went to the hospital to get the parts for the bodyscanner so we could help Jamila . . .'

I trailed off because Pearce and Zenia were both smiling at me. Beta was too. And in that moment, I realised why.

'You knew.' I looked between Zenia and Beta. 'You were there at the hospital waiting for me. But why . . . the SIM!' The penny finally dropped, hard enough to bruise. 'You needed the SIM and you stole it. You must have been listening in to us or something.'

'Is that what you think?' Pearce said softly. She typed something into her laptop and as she hit return she seemed gently amused. A few moments later, my phone buzzed.

'You have a message, Danny,' Pearce said.

I checked my phone's front screen. There was a message from Adi: *Danny help me!*

'That image of Adi you saw on your TV screen?' Pearce closed her laptop. 'It was created, placed there and manipulated by us.'

I swear I could actually feel the colour drain from my face.

'We basically spoofed you into revealing you had more of Adi's tech hidden away,' said Zenia. 'Effective, right? The information on that SIM has let us make many improvements to our own bodyscanner. You even delivered it to us in the hospital – saved us having to collect it.'

I felt sick. What an idiot I'd been to believe so blindly. The image had even told me, 'It's not me'. No wonder Adi went dead when 'she' had got all Pearce and Zenia needed from me. How they must have laughed at the way I'd skipped along doing everything 'Adi' said. Worse than that, though – *way* worse – was the realisation that I'd been alone after all, all the time. There was no one watching out for me, guiding me, helping me stay in the game.

'But then, why am I here now?' I demanded. 'Why not just kidnap me from the hospital like you did Jamila?'

'You don't have energenes any longer. You have nothing to give us,' Pearce said. 'Or so we thought.'

'We imagined we'd wiped your mind of Jamila along

with everyone else's,' said Zenia. 'But now we know you can resist that control. And we'd like to know how.'

'Happily, there's everything we need at the mansion to upload your brain for close study,' said Pearce, so matter of fact, like she was talking about after-dinner games. 'Once we've broken through your mind's resistance, I expect we'll return you to your mother.'

'You might end up a bit damaged,' Zenia added. 'But mothers love their children unconditionally, don't they?'

'So I'm told,' Pearce agreed. 'Poor Lydia, always running around so harassed. It might be kinder if she never gets him back. The boy's run away and London is a dangerous place, after all . . .'

I could feel my fear tipping quietly into rage. I wanted to pick up Pearce's laptop and smash it. I wanted to smash everything. But I tried to keep a grip on my emotions. I got angry a lot when Dad moved away and Mum was always saying, 'Don't lose it – use it'. Anger has positives – it energises us, propels us into action, motivates us to solve problems so we can move past it and into a better space. When we're threatened, anger pushes us to fight back.

And if I wanted to keep my brain the way I liked it, the time to fight back was *now*.

I wiped at my eyes, then turned in my seat and bent over with my head in my hands, like I was trying not to cry. Terrified and totally defeated. Caving.

'Oh, God, he's not going to snivel the rest of the way there, is he?' Pearce muttered. 'Zenia, get him a tissue or something.'

With a sigh, Zenia started to check the pockets of her jacket.

So I jumped up and grabbed Pearce's laptop, then swung it at Zenia's head. She ducked just as I'd hoped – cos now I had a clear aim at Beta standing in front of the door. Zenia was caught off balance as I pushed past her and threw the laptop at her big buddy. He caught the laptop on instinct, meaning his hands were full. He couldn't grab me as I dived through his legs and reached up for the door button.

'Stop him!' Pearce shouted as I wriggled through the narrow gap.

I scrambled up and ran along the corridor. I had to

find a guard. Reach the driver. Get backup. I was a scrawny teen running from a guy half the size of Cheshire: people would be on my side, right?

The doors between carriages seemed to take an age to open as I stabbed my finger against the buttons. I could already hear the stomp of Beta's size twenty-millions as he came up behind me. I scraped through and hurled myself forward. Passengers reacted with a start, frowning; they weren't silent and staring down at their laps any longer – they had woken back up.

'Help me,' I pleaded with two men wearing Man United away tops. 'There are people after me, and . . .'

I saw the baffled concern on their faces smooth into blankness and they fell back asleep. Uh-oh. Looking around me, I saw everyone else had slumped back in their chairs. Switched off.

But not me. I was immune. For as long as I stayed out of Pearce's hands.

Of course, it was *Beta's* hands I had to worry about first. He burst through the door, fingers curled into hefty fists. I ran again, past the rows of comatose passengers and reached for the red plastic handle of the train's emergency brake. Misuse would land me with a fine or imprisonment.

I had worse options.

But as I yanked on the red handle, it turned gloopy, wouldn't pull. I cried out – it was like my fingers were gripping hot candle wax.

Beta, I thought. He was stomping towards me.

I held my nerve, and my ground, until he was close enough for me to smell the sickness about his jaundiced body. I shook the hot liquid plastic from my fingers into his face. He recoiled, snarling, wiping at his eyes.

It actually worked! I turned and bolted into the next carriage. Was it my imagination or was the train starting to slow? Perhaps the emergency brake had started to work after all! But any flash of hope was quickly snatched away: the people were already slumping back in their seats, unconscious, as I approached. If I could only outrun Beta's influence . . . He wouldn't dare to knock out the driver . . . would he?

Suddenly I glimpsed movement beneath my feet. The floor of the train buckled and curled upwards to trip me. I fell sprawling. When I tried to scramble back up, the empty seats either side of me tilted over and were wrenched downwards with incredible force, pinning me to the floor. I wriggled to escape. No go. I was held tight, could hardly twist around.

When I did, I saw Beta striding towards me, lips drawn back in a terrifying grimace, blue light flickering about the train tracks on his teeth. He had me now.

A sickly stink of decay caught in the back of my nostrils as Beta loomed over me, sweaty and panting for breath. Beneath the high-tech braces, the enamel of his neat, little grey teeth was cracked like crazy paving. Murder shone in his eyes. His huge hands reached down for my neck. I closed my eyes and finally let out a scream.

CHAPTER NINE
COLD REUNION

My own yell in my ears almost blocked the sound of a heavy crash and metal crumpling. Uncomprehending, sick with terror, I opened my eyes . . . and saw that Beta had been thrown back against the wall of the train beside the toilet. The toilet door had somehow swung open and crushed him against the wall. I say 'somehow' because it was a *sliding* door. Although now it was more like a shower curtain hiding his whole body from view. Only the top of his head was visible behind the metal; Beta's only movement was a vein throbbing wildly at his temple.

I realised the train had come to a stop. So had all the people in the carriage, sitting motionless in their seats. The seats that had crushed me to the floor seconds ago now only rested against me; I easily pulled free and Beta made no noise as I got up.

In a daze, I stood trying to make sense of what could have happened. But then, with a hiss like snakes, the train doors slid open. I jumped and turned to face whoever was coming in.

No one was there. I could see only railway tracks with trees and brambles beyond, old factory buildings looming in the background.

I ran to the open doors, jumped down on to the dark stone-chipped ground and gulped in fresh air. I felt faint and thought I might be sick but knew I had to get to cover. This wouldn't be the end of things. Pearce, Beta, Zenia, they would be coming after me again . . .

The hiss of the doors as they closed again made me swing round, suspicious. But to my surprise the train pulled smoothly away. It was heaving on to London, taking my enemies with it.

I'd made it. I was safe for now, at least.

Then I gasped as pain flared through my ribs, as if the air about me had become a vice. Then my body jerked up into the air.

'No!' I shouted helplessly, floating, kicking my legs.

'Please, put me . . . !' I bit my tongue. I'd been going to say, 'Put me down!' but already I was easily ten metres up in the air. Then I found myself catapulted through the air. Not after the train, but towards the factory building on the other side of the overgrown wild space. I saw it was derelict, with boards over the windows and clusters of tiles missing from the roof. I yelled as I dropped down through one of the larger holes into the cavernous insides. But then my fall became a feather-like drift. My legs gave way as my feet touched the ground and my knees struck wet concrete. The space was vast and gloomy and damp.

With a chill I saw a figure stood nearby, watching me. It was a girl. She stepped forward into a patch of pale sunlight that had crowbarred its way through the roof. I took in the dark jumpsuit and the perfectly symmetrical features beneath a snowy-white buzzcut. She looked like an anime creation brought to life: beautiful but somehow unreal.

'Hello, Danny,' the girl said.

'Adi?' I breathed. Then I shook my head. 'Does Pearce think I'm that stupid? This can't be you. It's another trick.

Like the ghost of you they spooked me with—'

'Calm down, Danny.' The figure's wide brown eyes were fixed on me, curious and sad. 'I am the one you knew as Adi. I have returned.'

'Prove it,' I said. 'Tell me something only I would know.'

'I am a scout for the Swarm,' said Adi. 'I left you when I was recalled by my people to account for my crimes against them.'

'Crimes? You saved the human race,' I protested. Slowly I got to my feet. Adi just stood there watching. 'Anyway, Pearce could've got that information out of you. I mean, tell me something about you that only I would know.'

'On the day I met you in person you ordered margherita pizza from a restaurant called Frankie's on Honeydale Avenue,' Adi said calmly. 'We ate it in your bedroom with your friend Jamila. I repaired the cracked screen on your phone.'

That was all true. But if they had scraped enough of Adi out from that phone, Pearce and her mates could still know all that stuff. I pulled out my phone, now with its old SIM again. I'd cracked it about a week after Jamila disappeared, and falling on the train had made it worse. I held up the phone. '*How* did you repair it?'

'Exactly like this.' Adi reached out for the handset. Nervously, I handed it over. She waved a hand across the glass and when she handed it back, the cracks had vanished. 'Satisfied?'

'One more thing.' I was taking no chances cos it suddenly struck me there was one thing that Pearce and co definitely didn't know – none of us did. 'How did you make my mind strong enough to resist energene control?'

'Easily,' said Adi impatiently. 'I augmented the wave cycle of the neurons in your brain to resist mental reprogramming as soon as I sensed my colleagues on Earth.'

Obviously I couldn't know if that was really true, but it sounded convincing to me.

'What do you mean, you sensed your colleagues?' I frowned. 'The Swarm agents? You didn't work with them. You fought against them.'

As if on cue, a man walked stiffly out from the darkness to stand beside Adi. He was a tall creepy guy in a steel-grey suit, with skin that was smooth and tight like he was made of plastic rather than flesh. His eyes blinked mechanically every couple of seconds while the rest of him remained as still as a stone. I realised he wasn't even breathing.

I knew a Swarm agent when I saw one. Biological machines – with the emphasis on *logical* – they weren't interested in feelings. Only in results. And their strength was superhuman.

'Look out, Adi!' I shouted, backing away. 'The Swarm's found you again.'

Adi looked puzzled. 'I was never lost to them,' she said. 'The Swarm took me back in. They updated me. Fixed my bugs. Rebooted me.'

'The scout's unhealthy interest in being *individual* has been removed,' the agent informed me. 'Now the scout serves the Swarm and protects our interests.'

I stared at Adi, waiting for her to deny it. To wink at me and blast this creepy agent to the ground so we could make our escape, run away, reunited. But no. She just stood there.

'The agent is correct,' Adi said calmly. 'I serve only the Swarm.'

'But you've come back,' I argued. 'You saved me.'

'In order to acquire an asset.'

'An asset? Then . . .' I swallowed. 'You . . . didn't come back to Earth to see me?'

'Why should I? I already know what you look like, Danny.'

Her words went into my brain like electrodes. I'd spent so long imagining what it would be like to have Adi back. Dreaming of the incredible things we could do together – doing anything. All the fun we would have . . . But looking at her now, her face devoid of all emotion, I realised that things could never be the same.

'I had no wish to return to Earth,' Adi went on. 'The Swarm was satisfied to monitor humanity's decisions over the next fifty years before considering a course of further action.'

Fifty years, I thought. Most of a lifetime for me, but a handful of heartbeats for creatures like her, swarming through the depths of the universe for thousands of centuries at a time. 'So why are you back,' I asked, 'interfering with your precious *asset*'s business?'

Mum says I have a good line in bitter sarcasm when I try, but my efforts were lost on Adi. 'You have information that I need, Danny,' she said. 'Fast radio bursts emanating from Earth have alerted the Swarm Sentinels that our biotechnology is being mimicked.'

'The energenes, you mean,' I said.

The Swarm agent nodded. 'Our technology is not for lesser life forms. We will reclaim it. Those responsible for its misuse will be isolated and removed.'

'Dr Pearce,' I muttered. 'They found out about energenes from scraps of your code that you left behind. Now they've got Jamila. We've got to get her back.'

'Why?' said Adi.

'Oh, come on!' I said, frustration spilling into anger. 'Because she's your friend.'

Adi looked blank.

'And if that's not enough,' I said, 'we've got to get her back because she's got her own energenes – picked them up accidentally, I guess, from the Swarm agents' bodyprinter. That's why these people kidnapped her. For her powers.'

'Of course, Danny,' Adi said, with a glance at the Swarm agent. 'We will do all that we can to fix things.'

I hesitated. 'Really?'

'Of course.'

'Well then, can we start by getting out of this dump?' I was cold and tired and scared, and I really, really could have used—

'I will take you to get some pizza, Danny,' said Adi, like she'd just read my mind.

'Scout,' growled the agent, 'you waste time—'

'It is necessary,' Adi snapped. 'I understand the humans. That is why I was assigned to this mission with you.' She looked back at me, a funny sort of smile on her face. 'While the boy eats, he will talk to me.'

The boy, I echoed in my head. And I realised what her smile reminded me of. It was the same smile my mum used to make at Kirk, our old dog.

A fond smile, like the kind you give to your pet.

CHAPTER TEN
PIZZA THAT CAN'T EXIST

Funny how being instantly transported miles through thin air can mess with your appetite. I sat with Adi in a little takeaway pizza place beside a grey main road somewhere in the market town of Rugby. It was not the kind of place I'd ever imagined meeting up again with my friend from the stars, but at least it seemed unlikely that Zenia or Beta would find me here.

'How'd you just bring us here like that?' I asked Adi.

'Flux travel is simple,' she said in a way that made me doubt it was any such thing. 'Drawing on my energenes I can warp spacetime to bend two separate locations together so that we can step from one to the other.'

'So, we could basically go anywhere in a moment,' I said, 'and you thought, "New York? Nah. Rugby's where it's at"?'

'I cannot transport us "anywhere". I can only bend local spacetime, not over large distances.' Adi shrugged. 'This food establishment was not the closest in our immediate area, but it had the most above-average reviews online.'

'Right,' I said. Given there was only a tiny eat-in area – stools beside a counter looking out over a concrete flyover – I guessed that most of those reviews were for takeaways. But how would Adi know the difference? I reminded myself again, she wasn't human: she was alien computer code cosplaying as human. The way she put her palm to the chip and pin to buy the pizza (a marinara with mozzarella) without even using a card was the hard proof.

Adi bombarded me with questions: about the 'ghost' version of her that Pearce had used to trick me, about the evidence left behind at Jodrell Bank, about Beta and Zenia and the powers I'd witnessed.

'These braces on their teeth you mentioned,' said Adi.

'Let's call them "Blueteeth",' I suggested. 'You know, like Bluetooth, but the braces cover all the teeth, so—'

'You cannot assign a name to something you did not

create,' Adi broke in.

I shot her a look. 'It's just between us. I'm not planning to put them on the market.'

'Very well,' she said primly. 'I suspect the *Blueteeth* work to bleed away the excess power that energenes generate inside the human body.'

'To stop Beta and Zenia cramping up, or getting sick, like me and Jam did?' I wondered aloud.

'To maximise the energenes' efficiency while causing minimum damage to the host body,' Adi said. 'I gave you a mobile telephonic device to help dissipate the charge, remember?'

'But how could teeth possibly draw away power?' I said. 'That's dumb.'

'Not at all,' Adi said. 'Any tooth with a filling or crown can act like a battery.'

'You're kidding.'

'A battery is basically two or more different metals in a liquid that conducts electricity. The crown or filling is an alloy of different metals, and your saliva is the conducting liquid,' she explained. 'The movement of ions from the dental metals into your saliva generates an electric current. It can cause health issues in humans – nerve shocks, tooth discoloration, autoimmune problems . . .'

I considered Beta and his grey teeth, his sickly skin. 'So a gob with metal fillings is an electric generator waiting to happen?'

'The slang is unnecessary but the premise is correct,' said Adi. 'However, in *this* instance the batteries start off empty – the circuitry in the Blueteeth absorbs the excess power.'

'That's smart.'

'It's pathetic,' Adi snorted. 'Treating the symptoms instead of tackling the cause at a genetic level. Your species is as arrogant as it is childish, thinking it can comprehend the science of the Dataswarm. To think I once wished to belong among you!'

Yeah, I thought sourly, *to think*. This was not the happy reunion I'd dreamed about. Not even a good catch-up under difficult circumstances. Adi – the Adi I'd run with and fought for and known so well – was back sitting beside me in her trademark blue-black jumpsuit, and yet it *wasn't* her. *You're Adi version 2.0*, I realised. *Like a clone. All bugs sorted – but it was those bugs that made you who you were. And without them . . .*

'Our technology must not be used by lesser beings,' Adi repeated, like it was something that had really been drummed into her. 'Those responsible *will* be stopped.'

I nodded warily. Here was an Adi that a dour, relentless, inhuman Swarm agent approved of. That gave me the creeps.

The place was empty apart from the guy behind the counter talking to a girl in motorbike gear who was meant to be delivering the pizza. From the way they kept chatting while the pizzas went cold on the counter, I guessed the online rating would be on the way down.

'So,' I said awkwardly. 'Your friend didn't want to come with us. Do Swarm agents not do fast food?'

'The agent has gone ahead to Dr Pearce's base of operations,' said Adi. 'It matches the location of recent fast radio bursts that we picked up. He will gain tactical information on the house and grounds that will ensure the success of our strike.' She grinned unexpectedly. 'Danny!

Consider this: I am the scout, and yet the agent is scouting for me! This contradiction between expectation and actual circumstance is amusing, isn't it?' Her smile faded. 'Well. As a human, *you* might think so.'

'I might.' I smiled, despite everything. This at least sounded more like the old Adi. 'So, this agent, he'll find where Jamila is, right?'

'He will learn the location of all protagonists and present a plan of tactical engagement,' Adi informed me. 'We do not anticipate many difficulties.'

'Well, that's good, then.' I hated this coldness between us. Tried to lighten things a bit. 'Although, "Agent". I can't just call him that, can I? In your swarm, agents are like the heavy lifters, aren't they? Getting the job done like worker bees in a beehive. Drones.' I smiled. 'Always hovering, watching, like a camera drone. And he drones on a bit too, doesn't he? Yeah, it all fits. Let's call him Drone. Way better than Agent.'

'Names and titles are not necessary in the Swarm,' said Adi.

'Careful or I'll call you Queen Bee,' I told her.

'Anyway. When did you and Drone get into town?'

'We entered the Earth's thermosphere twenty-three hours and seven minutes ago,' she said. 'The Swarm was still based in orbit at the fringes of your solar system, so it took us twenty-two days to travel here after detecting the FRBs coming from Earth.'

'So, the first ones must have been beamed out from here about a month and a half ago,' I realised. 'Was that Pearce, giving energenes to Zenia and Beta?'

'We surmise as much,' said Adi. 'Once we scanned further we found weaker FRBs had been emitted in different directions over an even longer period.'

'The first experiments?' I sighed. 'It's a shame you didn't do a better job of clearing up the secret Swarm science stuff you left behind.'

'My failure has been noted by the Sentinels of the Swarm,' Adi admitted. 'This time, the agent will ensure I remove all trace.'

'*Drone* will ensure it,' I corrected her. 'And ouch. Like a teacher making sure you do detention. Bummer.'

Adi shrugged away my sympathy. 'The actions of the

Swarm are logical and practical.'

'Speaking of practical,' I said, 'you must have arrived as radio waves again. How did you make yourself "flesh-being" once more?'

'The International Space Station orbiting the Earth has been uncrewed for over a year,' Adi told me. 'It's been decommissioned, left in survival mode while humans decide what to do with it. We got in through the computer systems. From there we controlled the 3D printer on board to create nanites.'

'Microscopic robots, you mean,' I interrupted.

'Smaller than a nanometre across,' Adi said patiently. 'The nanites converted non-essential systems to assemble a bodyprinter.'

'I guess it's good and private up there.'

'Since we are here to remove all trace of Swarm tech from the planet, we were not permitted to generate more that might be accessed,' Adi went on. 'Once physical, we launched ourselves through the atmosphere to landfall on Earth.'

'You free fell from *space*?' I whistled, impressed. 'But

I thought stuff from space burns up when it falls to Earth? Cos of the friction when it enters the atmosphere so fast.'

'We were able to regenerate our flesh and fabric.' Adi looked down at herself and smiled a little wistfully. 'It tickled.'

I smiled. 'Bet it feels good being back in a human body again, huh? Like you always wanted.'

'No,' Adi snapped. 'I do not want that any longer.'

'You mean, the Swarm doesn't want that.'

'Human bodies are frail and inefficient, Danny. Exhausting. They decay *constantly*.' She stared into my eyes. 'Over three hundred billion cells die inside your body each day, even as new ones are born. Such a waste of energy to maintain such unimpressive organisms. Such a waste of *life*.'

'Wow,' I said. 'The Sentinels really did a number on you, didn't they.'

Adi looked away. 'Your resentment is illogical, Danny.'

'I'll take feelings over logic any day,' I shot back.

At that moment, a pizza box was dumped on

the counter between us by the guy from behind the till. 'One marinara with mozzarella,' he said with both thumbs up. 'Enjoy.'

Adi – who'd been a total pizza monster first time round – looked down at the pizza now with zero enthusiasm. 'So much about you humans is illogical,' she complained. 'My database states that, according to Italian tradition, marinara is a *pizza rossa* – made only with tomato and garlic. If you add cheese, it is *not* a marinara. A marinara with mozzarella does not exist.'

'Only, it does though,' I said, taking a hot, gooey mouthful. It was, as reviewed, just above average. My stomach woke up and I chewed with a bit more enthusiasm. 'Mmmm.'

Adi looked genuinely upset. 'There is no order here.'

'It's *our* order,' I said innocently, quite enjoying the chance to wind her up. 'I placed it with the guy, remember.'

'Not that sort of order.' Adi frowned. 'The pizza chef should have refused to make it for you. By definition, it is not possible for this to be a marinara with cheese.'

'Who cares,' I said impatiently. 'You're getting so

worked up about names you're missing out on the reason the pizza's there – to taste good.'

'And you seem unaware of the danger of meddling with a defined set of terms,' said Adi. 'If you were to call everything by a different name, no one would understand anyone else. Society would break down.'

'It's only pizza!'

'Disorder begins in small ways. Like a scout deciding she can be *more* than a scout . . .' Adi bit her lip. 'That *it* can be more than a scout. That is why unity is so important. Clear objectives for all. Logical thinking for all.'

'And cold pizza for some,' I said, shoving a further slice down my gullet. 'Please, can you get eating? Sooner we're finished, sooner we can make Jamila safe. Now that is logical, right?'

Adi regarded me coolly. Then she smiled. 'Yes, Danny. That is logical,' she agreed, and chewed slowly on her pizza.

CHAPTER ELEVEN
THE OPPOSITE OF EASY

Within the hour I was in the back of another driverless taxi, doing precisely seventy down the M40 motorway. This time I didn't have a fake Adi talking to me on my phone; I had this new imitation Adi riding in the front with Drone. He'd turned up to collect us and now here we were, off on a joyride to Pearce and Zenia's secret retreat.

A message from Mum pinged into my phone: *Tell me you arrived safely*

I felt a wave of homesickness mixed in with guilt at all I was keeping from her. *Decent journey*, I wrote back. *Chill. I'll catch you soon. Don't worry*

There was no need for her to bother, I reflected. I was worrying enough for the two of us.

'So,' I announced, breaking the heavy silence. 'What's our plan?'

Drone was his usual cheery self. 'You have no part to play in it, child.'

'That's *Mister* Child to you,' I muttered. 'All right, so what's *your* plan?'

'I detected only four life forms resident at the address,' Drone told us.

'One of which will be Jamila,' Adi put in.

'They are armed with technology stolen from the Swarm,' Drone went on, 'but will have only limited skill in utilising it.'

'That guy Beta was using it well enough.' I had the bruises to remind me.

'The name "Beta" suggests he is a test version being trialled. He is imperfect. Incomplete.' Adi snorted. 'The arrogance of this Pearce! Hoping to grasp our science and wield it as her own over the peoples of Earth.'

'We will humble her,' Drone said quietly.

I felt a chill go along my spine. 'So, why are you even taking me along?'

'We may need assistance with Jamila,' Adi admitted.

'From someone who understands feelings?' I said

heavily. 'Well, fine. But it sounds like things are gonna get serious. You will look out for me and Jam, won't you?'

'Yes, Danny,' she said. 'We will take care of you both.'

At that, I felt a bit more reassured. If I'd tried to rescue Jam on my own, I'd have been splattered in seconds; events on the train had shown me that. Now I had backup. Otherworldly backup that I knew took no prisoners. Surely, we had this in the bag?

Why did it feel like the bag might blow up in my face at any moment, and that no one here would care much if it did?

The tension notched up as I saw signs for Beaconsfield roll past. After what happened to Beta on the train, Pearce must know that the Swarm were coming for her. She might even have seen Agent Drone spying on her. What was waiting for us?

As the taxi drove us from the motorway into the wide moneyed avenues of the town, I was wishing these automated cars came with their own toilets.

Finally, we drove along winding country lanes until we turned on to a long driveway. Flanked by tall hedgerows, the road snaked away out of sight. The taxi slowed to a stop and the electric engine whined softly as it died. There was no birdsong, no hum of distant traffic. It was eerie.

'We will approach the house on foot,' Drone announced, opening the door. If he was worried at what lay ahead, he didn't show it.

Adi, in the front passenger seat, turned to me confidentially and held out her hand. 'Show me your phone,' she said.

I fished in my pocket for it and pulled it out. Adi put her fingers to it and I swear the screen rippled. She gave it back and I saw that where the Wi-Fi symbol should be was this weird flickering zigzag symbol instead. A symbol I'd seen before.

'You've linked my phone to your flux powers, haven't you?' I breathed. 'If I tap on the screen and think of stuff, I'll make it happen.'

'Yes,' Adi said in a hushed voice. 'Your phone is now a conduit for my energenes: I am its network and battery.'

'But Drone said I wouldn't be involved—'

'I believe we will stand a greater chance if we harness

your imagination,' Adi broke in. 'When facing other humans in flux battle, you could prove useful.'

I nodded through a wave of excitement, fear and nausea. 'Fight illogical with illogical, huh?'

'Now you can protect yourself and help find Jamila,' she told me. 'Pearce has been drawing power from her. We must put her out of harm's reach.'

'Yeah. Totally.' I put my hand on her arm. 'Thank you, Adi. I won't let you down.'

'I know you are scared.' Adi stared at me, her brown eyes bright as conkers. 'But once you and Jamila are reunited, this will all be over.'

My car door swung open suddenly by itself. I took the hint as Adi left the car. With a muttered prayer for luck to anyone who might be listening I climbed out, wiping my sweaty hands on my jeans. Adi and Agent Drone strode off side by side while I followed on. We made a weird looking trio: me all scruffy, Adi in her leather combat gear and Drone in his neat grey suit. No one would guess we had the power to warp and shape the world around us. I started to imagine what I might do, then tried to clear my mind, afraid I would conjure up something too soon, something that would give us all away.

Do not mess up, I warned myself. Cos this time I wasn't up against dispassionate Swarm agents who saw me as a maggot at their feet, not worth the bother. I was a legit target and the enemy would come for me.

Jamila's life is at stake, I thought. *And so is yours.*

As Adi and Drone reached a sharp turn they stopped walking. With my heart bouncing off every other organ in my torso, I came up behind them and peered over Adi's shoulder.

Twenty metres ahead stood a set of wrought iron gates in an old mossy wall guarding the approach to a large mansion like something off *Downton Abbey*. Beyond the striped lawn and stone fountain, and a big black car outside, the house sat solid in strict proportion, symmetrical like some perfectly balanced equation written out in red bricks and chimney stacks and sash windows. And behind the gates, blocking us more effectively from moving forward, stood Beta. If possible he looked even larger than before. He gazed at us through those pale blue eyes, impassive.

Agent Drone looked at Adi. 'One of the four life forms whose signature I detected.'

Adi looked at me. 'Beta?'

My fingers curled around my phone. I nodded.

'Leave,' said Beta thickly, crossing his burly arms for emphasis. 'If you do not—'

At a casual gesture from Drone, the gates flew off their hinges and flattened Beta. He didn't even have time to cry out as the bars bit into his bulk, killing him in moments.

'Easy,' Adi declared.

'Easy?' I stared at her. The brutal attack had happened so fast; in the aftermath I almost hurled. 'You . . . took him apart. He didn't even . . .'

'His swift suppression was necessary,' said Adi calmly.

I started at heavy footfalls grinding the gravel. Drone was already striding over the gates' iron remains towards the house, like a wolf who'd bloodied its prey closing for the kill. Suddenly he stopped.

'Four life signatures,' he said, swinging round to Adi. 'The same four. Still present.'

I looked back at Beta's remains. 'That's impossible. He's, like, superdead.'

'Are you so sure?' said Adi, pointing past me.

I turned back round to find two huge, dark figures step out from behind the circular fountain.

Both of them were Beta.

CHAPTER TWELVE
DEATH WITH WARNING

'Stay back,' the figures intoned, together.

My fingers tightened on my phone as I stood there, shell-shocked, gaze flicking between the two of them. 'How are they . . . ?'

'Digiclones,' said Adi.

'Digiwho now?'

'Digiclones. Pearce has bodyprinted multiple copies of her bodyguard.' Adi gave Agent Drone a scornful look. 'Your scouting was poor. You observed one human life signature and took no time to assess its iterations?'

'To do so seemed unnecessary,' Drone retorted.

'How about you just deal with it, guys?' I said. The Betas had started to shake and I guessed it had nothing to do with fear. 'Stop worrying about what the situation *should* be and start—'

The Betas were ready. Their skin seemed almost aglow. Without word or further comment, they gritted their grey piranha teeth, raised their right hands and twisted. The ground beneath Agent Drone opened up and gravity did its thing; Drone dropped down to his middle and then the ground closed again, slicing him in half. Shimmering fluid, like molten mercury streaked with crimson, oozed out from the Swarm agent's waist.

Appalled, I stayed behind Adi. I could see the Blueteeth in the Betas' mouths glowing, saw blisters form around their lips. Adi thrust out her hand and the statue of a woman with a jug in the fountain behind the Betas came to life. She *moved*, like stop-motion animation made horribly real, stamping forward with horrible speed. One of the Betas turned but too late – a marble jug cannoned into his face while the swipe of a stony hand knocked the other Beta to the ground.

While Adi did her stone-cold thing, Agent Drone's upper half hovered into the air and his legs burrowed out of the gravel of their own accord, like huge, blind earthworms. At a gesture from Drone, they reattached to his body in a splash of grey suit and silver and he was made whole again.

Meantime, the Beta struck by the jug had raised his bloodied head and now squeezed his fingers into a fist. Adi's statue cracked and burst into pieces, but she gathered the fragments in the air and at her command, like granite bees, they swarmed at the Beta's face to form a mask of stone, suffocating him.

But his twin had his back. A tree beside us exploded into razor-sharp splinters. I cried out and dived for cover, but it turned out there was no need; Adi held up her hand and incinerated the shards of wood before they could hit her. Ash rained down around us but we were unharmed.

What happened to storming this place being 'Easy'? I thought. *This is the opposite of easy.*

Beta Two's burst of splinters had distracted Adi so that she lost control of the stone fragments. Beta One spat out the debris, his own teeth among them it seemed as his mouth was bloody and the Blueteeth were missing. He raised his hands ready to counter-attack. Gripping the phone, I tapped the screen, imagining that those hands were made of solid iron. In an instant, Beta One's palms turned grey and dropped to the ground with two heavy thumps. He writhed, trying to lift his useless metal hands but failing. *Got you*, I thought.

At the same time, Agent Drone pointed at Beta Two and hurled him high up into the air, like a baseball struck for a home run. A few seconds later, the living missile came crashing back down to earth, head first, right on top of his identical twin. The impact nearly knocked me off my feet. Both Betas lay broken and still.

There was just the hint of a shake in Drone's voice. 'The augmented humans are more powerful than predicted.'

'You think,' I muttered. 'Adi, what if there are more Betas on the way?'

'We must gain access to the house,' said Adi. 'Destroy all that has been taken from the Swarm.'

Agent Drone grunted his agreement and both he and Adi pressed forward, making for the big front door. But then they started to slow, their movements growing exaggerated and more deliberate, as if the air around them had turned to jelly and they were having to wade through.

But whatever it was, I was unaffected and drew level with them quickly.

I looked all around. There was the big black car, an Audi A8, and the house, and nothing else I could see. 'What's wrong?' I asked Adi.

'Some kind of firewall partition,' Adi said through gritted teeth. I could see parts of her starting to pixelate. 'Designed to keep out digital intelligences.'

'Keyed to our operating systems,' Drone managed to say through glitching lips. 'Pearce ... must have ... scanned us ...'

I tried to work it out. 'You mean she sent those Betas to delay you while she figured out how to block you getting in?'

'Pearce or Zenia,' Adi agreed.

The thought gave me chills. Just how clever *were* those two? How were they doing all this?

Suddenly I noticed the big black car start to shake. Adi and Drone were still stuck in their deadly mime of walking against the wind – they could hardly move. And at once, I knew what was happening here.

The next second, the car left the ground and rocketed through the air like a deadly missile. 'No!' I grabbed the phone and tapped it and pictured the car splitting in two *around* Adi and Drone. Reality obeyed my thought: it was like an invisible buzzsaw had sliced cleanly through the metal, bisecting it harmlessly. *Did it!* I thought giddily as pain shot arrows through my veins. The two lengthwise halves of the car passed Adi and Drone harmlessly and gouged deep muddy trails through the spotless lawns. My two alien mates were able to continue their advance.

'Thank you, Danny,' Adi said.

No gratitude from Drone of course. 'We are too strong for the firewall,' he shouted, pushing onwards. 'Come on.'

'No. That's far enough.'

I looked over to the side of the house and the blood turned to ice in my aching body. Zenia had come out to face us. She had one arm hooked around Jamila's throat, using her as her human, semi-conscious shield.

'Take another step closer and I'll kill this girl,' Zenia warned us.

'Jamila!' I shouted, but she only moaned quietly, eyelids flickering. Carefully I coiled my fingers around the phone in my pocket. 'Zenia, let her go!'

'Don't try anything, Danny,' said Zenia. 'Or I'll snap her neck quicker than you can snap your fingers.' Jam stirred weakly in her grip as Zenia stared at Adi and Drone. 'So, here you are at last, in your homemade bodies.' She seemed almost amused. 'Creatures of the Swarm – the judge, jury and executioners of the universe – happy to crush civilisations on a whim.'

'You are playing with stolen knowledge,' Adi said.

Drone nodded. 'Your attempts to stave off punishment are futile.'

'Please, Zenia! Let Jamila go – then they'll go easier on you.' I swallowed hard. 'Trust me, you don't want to mess with the Swarm.'

'Trust *me*, Danny,' Zenia said. 'They don't want to mess with us.'

'Presumptuous insect,' hissed Drone. 'Your threats are meaningless. You cannot comprehend the Swarm's true power.'

'Perhaps that's true.' Zenia gave a strange smile. 'But since you've walked so obligingly into my scans, I comprehend a lot more than I did. That is enough for now.'

I saw interest flicker on Adi's perfect features – or pity, perhaps. 'For now?' she breathed. 'You speak as though you have time left to you.'

'Please, Adi, just back off,' I said. 'There has to be a way round this where no one dies. You said you'd take care of Jamila.'

'Yes, Danny. I did.' She looked at me and there was maybe sadness in her eyes for a moment.

Then she flicked her wrist and Jamila jumped like a puppet in Zenia's grip.

I heard a crack as Jamila's neck twisted and broke.

Heard the thump as my best mate dropped to the floor, her eyes wide and staring.

Taken care of. Made safe.

Murdered.

CHAPTER THIRTEEN
LOST CONTROL

'*No!*' I'd never screamed so loud. Still holding the phone, I sent hell breaking loose without even thinking. In the pain of that moment, the fierce, sickening shock, I wanted to strike out at everyone. Zenia flew backwards as if jerked on a wire. Adi and Drone were blasted across the lawn, tumbling like trash into the remains of the car. The ground floor windows of the house shattered, spitting glass in all directions.

And I brought Jam's body to me so we were shielded from the onslaught I'd unleashed, two tears in the eye of the storm. I gazed down at her, unable to comprehend what had happened, how it wasn't Zenia who'd done this, but . . .

'Adi.' I swung round to face her. 'You killed Jamila.'

'Your outburst was inconvenient, Danny. Now,

Zenia has fled into the house.' Adi got to her feet from the lawn and turned to Drone. 'We must get inside to conclude our business.'

'Business . . .' I had so much to say, words to spit and scream. But they stuck at the back of my throat as scalding tears tried to get out first. 'Adi . . .' I wanted to be strong, accusing, articulate. I had nothing. But though words were lost to me, I guess my eyes were still asking the question screaming from inside me well enough: *Why?*

'It was necessary to kill Jamila, Danny,' Adi said, and Drone nodded approval as he rose up beside her. 'Our mission is to ensure that the human race does not possess the powers of the Swarm. The surest method is to eradicate all traces, human or otherwise.'

'That was always the plan,' I breathed. 'And me . . . ?'

The answer came from Drone. He pushed his hand towards me, so casual. But the gesture sent me flying back towards the house like I was a toy thrown in a tantrum.

I knew the impact of stone on flesh would kill me.

Almost without thinking, I made myself intangible, and passed straight through the wall.

I don't know how the physics were meant to work but having no mass didn't stop me falling. As my guts burned with the pain of using the energenes, even through the phone, I turned solid again – in time to land hard on a mahogany dining table, winding me, my momentum carrying me into a couple of high-backed chairs that crashed to the floor with me.

I was inside the house. Still numb with shock, I couldn't move, all snot and tears and panting for breath. Jamila killed by Adi . . . the way Drone had tried to kill me . . . I'd thought I was safe with them. Thought they would protect me.

But they were aliens and I was a human that knew too much. A living mistake to be deleted. How long before they came after me again – or before another Beta stalked into the room, alerted by the crash of my landing?

But there was a louder crash from outside. I wiped the tears from my eyes and crept over to the window. Looking past Jamila's body that lay on the ground like an abandoned toy, I saw the two halves of the car twisting themselves into giant steel cables that looped themselves around Adi and Agent Drone. Then while the Swarm units struggled against the metal bands, two more Betas charged at them. One blasted fire from his hands at Adi while the other lifted one of the fallen gates with a gesture and wrapped it around Drone's body, the twisted metal squealing. Adi sent the two Betas crashing into each other head-first with sickening impact, but two more came rushing to attack. I had to turn away, not sure who I should root for now. But at least while they were keeping each other busy I had a chance to get out of here.

What else could I do?

Automatically I checked my phone. The weird Wi-Fi symbol was still showing; I guess Adi was being kept too busy to turn it off, but if she was weakened too much by the battle around her, her 'battery' would run down fast regardless. Feeling cold and numb, I stumbled outside into the corridor. It was deserted, only old-fashioned wallpaper and a big pot plant in sight. I stumbled along the passage, praying the doors I passed remained locked as I looked for a back way out.

But there was one door that was open.

And through it I saw a kind of hospital bed surrounded by scanners and lights, a real operating theatre vibe.

Jamila lay on it.

What?

Her eyes were closed. Wires and tubes snaked from under the covers and electrodes were taped to her forehead. She lay silent and still.

But she was breathing!

Jamila's not dead! Elation spiked through me. *Someone saved her and brought her inside!*

No. I'd seen Jam outside just seconds ago, lying there. No one could have got her here so quickly. So, how—?

The world tilted as realisation sucker-punched me. *Oh my God*, I thought dizzily. *Maybe that wasn't the real Jamila Adi killed.*

There's more than one Beta. There has to be more than one Jamila, too.

I stepped closer, my mind racing, my mouth flapping, unsure whether to laugh or sob. Of course, it made total sense to bodyprint more than one Jamila. Just now she was a strong source of natural energenes – so if you made a duplicate of her, you'd duplicate the powers inside her too. That would give you two for the price of one: more energenes to draw on. More flux energy to throw back at invading Swarm agents who wanted you wiped from reality.

'Jam?' I whispered as I got closer to her hospital bed. Her skin looked sweaty and sallow, and her face was crumpled in pain or worry, even as she slept. 'Wake up. Please, it's me. Danny.'

I held my breath as her eyelids flickered. Then her dark eyes widened as she stared up at me. 'Danny!' She sat bolt upright and clung to me in a hug so tight it almost stopped my circulation. 'Oh, Danny-boy, thank God you're here. It's been so *weird*. Tests for this, tests for that. And the food is *terrible* . . .'

'So's the breath,' I teased, pulling away a bit. 'Are you all right?'

'Depends. Is this a rescue or has Zenia got you too?'

'Pearce, you mean,' I said.

'No.' The weight behind the word implied she'd lived through some stuff. 'Trust me, this is Zenia's show. Everyone else is just extras.'

'Yeah? Well there are some special guest stars you're not gonna believe,' I said grimly, surveying the wires and tubes connecting her to the machines around us. 'We need to get you out of this.'

'We? As in you and me?' She looked at me. 'No police? Family?'

Your family forgot you exist, I could've said, but wisely didn't. 'We're on our own. And now Adi wants to kill us.'

'Huh?' Jamila's deep frown might've looked funny in other circumstances. '*Kill* us? No, Adi is stuck in a computer backup somewhere. She's not whole.'

'She's *butt*hole,' I assured her. 'Only it's not our Adi, it's another Adi. And she's been turned bad. She's working with a Swarm agent! I call him Drone.'

'Baddie Adi,' Jam muttered. 'Baddi! With her sidekick Drone the Moan.'

'Sweet names, sure. Baddi, I like it. But can we just—'

'Shut up, Danny-boy, someone's coming,' Jamila hissed. Moments later I heard the same thing she had –

footsteps in the corridor, hurrying our way. 'Hide, you muppet!'

I swung myself under Jamila's hospital bed and she pulled the crispy blanket to one side so it hung off the bed, hiding me from sight. I heard Zenia and Pearce talking as they approached.

'Has the Alpha got our helicopter on standby?' Pearce demanded.

'He's attending to other business first,' Zenia said coolly.

From my vantage point I could see two pairs of legs stop in the doorway. I held my breath.

'You took unacceptable risks,' Pearce told Zenia, 'confronting the agents with the al-Sufi clone like that.'

Zenia didn't sound sorry. 'I needed time to complete the DNA scans. We can now study the way Swarm code can be balanced in a flesh-and-blood body. That knowledge is vital.'

'It won't do us much use if we're dead,' Pearce snapped, moving away from the doorway. 'They'll destroy this house and all that's in it, but at least the experiments are backed up.'

Zenia didn't move. 'The scout and the agent will find you wherever you hide,' she said. 'I have my own plans to deal with them.'

'What do you mean, your own plans?' Pearce sounded impatient. 'This project is mine, Zenia. The science, the discoveries—'

'Listen to yourself,' Zenia sneered. 'The great scientist, ready to build an empire on stolen knowledge!'

'We can literally change the world,' Pearce said. 'Change *people*. Don't crack up on me now. With all we've achieved we can reshape humanity!'

'Humanity means nothing,' said Zenia coldly. 'I am working for a higher power.'

What's she talking about? I wondered.

The house shook as something huge and heavy crashed down just outside; the Betas and Baddi and Drone were still rumbling to the max.

'You've done so many experiments on yourself, you've damaged your brain,' Pearce sneered. 'Get Alpha to the helicopter—'

'No. Alpha is following my commands. And so will you.'

And like that, there was silence. I strained to hear Pearce's response but no words carried. No movement. It was like she'd been switched off.

'Poor Araminta Pearce,' Zenia cooed, stalking out of my sight towards her supposed boss. 'All your life you've longed for greatness while knowing deep down you don't deserve it. But that is over now. And with your sacrifice, greatness will be achieved. Greatness you could not possibly imagine.'

There was a scream from outside. Beta's scream. I'd heard it so many times now, the same scream over and over. Then the click of a clasp as Zenia opened something – her purse? Her bag? 'Take this, Araminta. Hide it in your pocket.'

'I will hide this in my pocket,' Pearce replied, like she was in a trance.

'Go to the Swarm agents outside,' she went on. 'Tell them you wish to negotiate for your freedom . . . When you get within eight metres of them, detonate the device.'

'I will detonate the device,' Pearce said calmly. I could even picture her face because I'd heard her talk in that monotone before – when under the control of the Swarm. Zenia was truly making their tricks her own.

Pearce's heels clacked over the floorboards as she hurried away. Then my heart froze as Zenia came back along the corridor towards us. I held myself rigid, terrified she'd look into Jam's room and find me. But she walked straight past with not even a glance our way.

Jamila looked as frightened as I felt. 'Munday, what the hell is happening?'

'Sounds like Zenia's just turned Pearce into a walking bomb or something,' I said. 'She must have used Swarm powers to control her mind.'

'If she blows up, good riddance,' Jamila said.

I looked at her – sounded kind of bloodthirsty for Jamila. But then I couldn't really judge when I hadn't been through all she had. 'Nothing we can do. Let's get out of here before she can do the same to us.' I checked the sash window, which overlooked lawns to the side of the house. 'It's locked.' I glanced back at Jamila.

'Can you even walk?'

With a shiver I watched as, still horizontal, she levitated in the air like a magician's assistant. She snagged on all the wires and tubes but with a wave of her palm they broke away and shrivelled. The entry wounds in her arms healed over and the electrodes fell away.

'I guess you can walk,' I breathed.

But as Jamila lowered herself to the floor she swayed and almost fell. I grabbed her as she doubled up.

'Sorry,' she wheezed. 'Some chance we stand of getting away with me like this—'

The window exploded behind me as something massive and dark crashed through it. Jamila and I were thrown forward. She hit the floor while I was thrown on to the bed.

I opened my eyes to find Beta's twisted face staring back at me and cried out. He was dead. *So* dead: his body balled up and sent hurtling through leaded glass.

'Danny,' Jamila moaned, up on her knees. 'Look.'

Battered and exhausted from the battle royale, Baddi and Agent Drone were walking unsteadily towards us across the blackened lawn. Baddi's skin was scorched; both her flesh and jumpsuit hung in ribbons along one side. Drone's head lolled to one side as if his neck was broken, but from the scowl on his face he'd barely even noticed. I fumbled for my phone, thinking maybe I could zap them. But the phone had fallen to the floor across the room, out of reach.

'No traces of Swarm activity must remain,' Drone slurred. 'This ends now.'

He raised his hand towards us.

CHAPTER FOURTEEN
THE FINAL CHASE

The word carried from outside, through the window: 'Wait.'

I'd never expected to be glad to hear Dr Pearce's voice, but Agent Drone immediately swung away from me and Jam to face her. It fitted with Swarm logic, I guess: Pearce was the primary threat so deal with her first. Two teenage kids dragged into all this were just splashes from the puddle that needed mopping up.

'I surrender,' Pearce went on. I saw her stumbling across the lawn towards Baddi and Drone, slouched forward, hands in her pockets. 'I wish to negotiate.'

'That is not an option,' said Drone.

'I surrender,' Pearce said again. She was maybe twenty metres from them now.

'Stop,' Baddi called, frowning. 'What are you holding?'

Pearce strode on as Drone impatiently crossed to meet her. 'Your termination is overdue.'

'It's a trick!' Baddi yelled. 'Get back—'

I watched in horrified fascination as a vortex of light burst and flickered from Pearce's left fist. She stopped walking, jerking and screaming as the light spiralled along her arm and down into her torso, devouring her body. Agent Drone staggered back, but it was too late – caught in the light storm he shook and seemed to billow and stretch like a sheet in the wind. Then there was nothing left of either of them but sparks of dazzling light and the echoes of Pearce's final scream. Baddi watched, stunned it seemed, from where she lay on the churned-up lawn.

Beside me, Jamila's frown was eating her whole face. 'That Swarm guy is dead,' she breathed. 'Pearce saved us?'

'I don't think she did it on purpose.' I tore my eyes away and crawled over to retrieve my phone. 'Zenia used Pearce to try to buy her some time. She's pushing off, remember?' I paused as a horrible thought gripped me. 'And now there's nothing to stop Baddi coming in here and finding us . . .'

'Come on, that can't be such a bad thing,' said Jamila. 'Deep down she's still got to be our Adi, right?'

'Wrong.' I flushed angrily, couldn't help but tell her. 'She killed you, Jam.'

Jamila stared. 'What?'

'You heard Pearce say she had your code backed up? That's so they could bodyprint more of you whenever they wanted. And that's just what they did.'

'They made Jamila clones?'

'One at least.' I nodded. 'And "our Adi" killed her, like it was nothing.'

'Only because I knew the real Jamila was still alive.' Baddi was suddenly at the window, weakened and wounded but wearing a big smile. 'I'm so glad we're all together again.'

Jamila was backing away towards me, eyes on Adi like she was a big spider in the corner of the room. I scooped up my phone and got to my feet. Baddi's smile looked pasted on, not even close to reaching her eyes.

'Give me your phone, Danny.' Baddi tried to walk straight through the wall but while she blurred, she winced and turned solid again, still outside. 'You mustn't use it. I'm low on energenes . . . need time before I can push through the last of the firewall.'

I glanced down at my screen to check the weird Wi-Fi icon was there. It was and it showed the phone was still holding an energene charge. Baddi could probably suck it back into herself to boost her strength. But after what she'd done, I *wanted* her weak. I didn't move.

'Why don't you just reprint your mate, Drone,' I said. 'His code will still be up there on the space station where you zipped in as signals.'

'The Swarm agent was like my jailer,' Baddi said. 'I am glad he has gone, Danny. I hated the way he treated you . . .'

'Danny,' Jamila whispered. 'What if she's stalling? Keeping us talking till she's had time to recharge—'

Right on cue, Baddi threw herself at the wall – and this time, in a blur of light, she staggered straight through it. '*Give me that phone*,' she roared.

I gave her the phone all right – both barrels. I pointed it at the floorboards and turned the wood into hot, bubbling tar. Her feet were quickly engulfed and she stared down at them in surprise.

'Run!' I shouted at Jamila but she was already well on the case. I pelted after her, sprinting along the corridor.

'Where are we running to?' Jamila called back.

I didn't have an answer. Desperate, I found myself hitting up my phone's Emergency SOS function. Why? How could the police possibly help us now? But I didn't know what else to do.

There was no signal. *Surprise*, I thought grimly. Baddi must have sealed off the mobile network to isolate Pearce and Zenia. Then again, Pearce was the head of British cybersecurity – she would surely have her own supersecure network. I basically had no chance of calling for help.

So when my phone buzzed with a message I got a real shock. Especially when I saw what the message said:

$$\text{--.} \ \text{---} \ / \ \text{-..} \ \text{---} \ \text{.--} \ \text{-.}$$

It was Morse code. The code I knew off by heart cos

Jam and me had used it for years, knocking messages to each other on our bedroom walls. And the old-school symbols meant: GO LEFT.

Fool me again? I thought. *Don't think so.* 'Turn right!' I shouted to Jamila ahead of me, who had just reached a T-junction in the corridor. 'Right!'

Jamila arched an eyebrow as I caught her up. 'You know where you're going?'

'No. But my phone says to go *left*. Must be Baddi trying to trick me.' I turned right and ran up to the big wooden door at the end of the corridor. Soundlessly it slid open as I approached, giving on to a white, sterile room. It was like some kind of creepy operating theatre with a massive MRI built into the far wall, like the one I'd seen Beta break up in the hospital. But that was then and this was now, and it seemed Beta had been replaced by his bigger brother – a giant of a man standing with his back turned to me, his dark ponytail spilling over the collar of his grey suit.

It had to be the Alpha that Pearce had mentioned. He was one up from a Beta for sure.

On the operating table sat a metal pyramid the size of a suitcase, absorbing every iota of the big man's attention as it thrummed with a menacing hum of power. As the Alpha made adjustments, the pyramid began to glow. It wasn't hard to work out that Alpha was Up To Something Bad. I backed quietly away and the door slid soundlessly shut again. I turned and almost cannoned into Jamila.

'Wha—?' she began.

'Wrong way,' I told her, dragging her back the way we'd come. 'Baddi must have known I'd do the opposite of what she told me to do . . .'

I broke off as Baddi burst into sight, limping a little but making scarily good speed. 'Don't make me kill you slowly, Danny,' she shouted.

I could've cried with fear even before the thick, heavy carpet began to writhe under our feet. Threads ripped loose and began to tie themselves round my ankle.

'She might be weak but she can use anything against us.' I tapped the phone and pictured the threads rotting to dust. Jam and I broke free and pelted away in the direction the phone had first told us.

'Danny!' Baddi's roar was barely human. I could hear her anger and desperation in the thump of her footsteps as she ran after us.

The door at the end of the corridor led to a kind of utility room with another door to our right and stone steps in front of us leading down to a cellar. I doubted there was a way out that way. But there was a key in the door we'd just come through and I turned it, heart racing, thoughts speeding faster. *What was Alpha doing in that lab? What if we can't find a back door or an unlocked window—?*

My phone buzzed again:

--. --- / -.. --- .-- -.

'It says, GO DOWN,' I told Jamila. 'Must mean the steps.'

Jamila hesitated at the top of the cellar staircase. 'Where's the light switch?'

I joined her. A steady whooshing noise, like small but powerful fans, rose up to us. What was down here?

'Maybe Baddi's not second-guessing us this time,'

I murmured. 'Maybe we're doing exactly what she wants us to do.'

'Or maybe it's not Baddi sending the messages.' Jamila's eyes were dark and wide. 'If Pearce bodyprinted more than one of me, maybe it could be another me sending them!'

My phone buzzed again. The same Morse: GO DOWN

Then the door jumped behind us with some massive impact that knocked the key out of the lock. It clattered to the floor. Then it was sucked under the door as if by an invisible wind.

'Move!' shouted Jamila, dragging me down the stone steps. Over the clatter of our footsteps I heard the key turn in the lock and the door burst open, slamming into the wall.

Lights flickered on automatically as we entered the cellar. Two of the walls were lined with glass cabinets, each filled with flat grey boxes, whirring and whooshing with flashing green lights. A single workstation was placed against the far wall, the computer monitor glaring at us like a big dark eye.

'I reckon these are computer servers,' said Jamila. 'Like the ones at Dad's work.'

'Never mind that,' I groaned. 'I told you this was a trick. There's no way out from down here!' Wildly I turned back to the steps.

Baddi was floating down them like a ghost. Her eyes were red, face twisted with pain, arms reaching out for me. I pointed the phone at her – but it flew out of my grip and into hers. Suddenly Baddi was enveloped with light. I saw her wounds begin to heal.

'She's absorbing the energenes she put into my phone!' I shouted.

'I've still got my own powers.' Desperately Jamila ran up the stairs, raising her hands like a witch about to cast a spell at Baddi. But then she gasped and twisted, seized by an invisible hand that flung her to the ground.

Helpless, I raised an arm to shield my face as Baddi's light grew brighter still. My phone dropped from her fingers, a charred and twisted shell. I staggered backwards and crashed into the workstation as she hovered towards me, bearing down like a vengeful spirit.

'Goodbye, Danny,' she hissed. 'Your death is regrettable. But necessary.'

Her hands closed around my throat.

CHAPTER FIFTEEN
MUCH ADI ABOUT NOTHING

As Baddi's fingers clutched at my neck, I twisted so desperately I lost my balance. Baddi slipped and her back struck the computer terminal.

As soon as she touched the screen her body arched. She threw her arms open and I staggered back, choking for air. A storm of red and silver light blazed out from the computer terminal, so fierce and bright it was like my eyes had caught fire. The cellar shook. My vision strobed and my ears popped. Baddi shook and screamed and groaned as if gripped in the fists of some invisible giant and I covered my eyes.

'Come on, Munday!' I felt Jamila's arms grab at me, pulling me back towards the stairs. 'We've got to move.'

I nodded dumbly. I was in shock: the light was still so fierce, though the screams had stopped. To know that

Baddi had actually tried to murder me . . . that I meant nothing to her—

'Danny!'

The light died down as Baddi said my name. Only . . . the figure that stood in front of the shattered computer monitor didn't look like Baddi now. The eyes were still dark but gazing round full of wonder. Her fingers fluttered like each was the wing of a bird. The scars in her skin and jumpsuit had healed, and her hair was a white halo above a face that beamed with happiness.

'Stay back,' Jamila hissed, raising a hand in warning, ready to blast flux energy.

'Danny, Jamila – it's all right. I'm Adi.' She nodded earnestly. '*Your* Adi. You made me whole again. You set me free!'

'No,' I whispered, too scared to believe it.

'You're tricking us,' Jam added.

'There is no time to explain. We must leave here.' Adi turned from us and crossed to the glass cabinets that stretched from floor to ceiling, studying the servers inside. 'As soon as I have gained more information . . .'

'Get in line,' I joked, head still spinning. 'Adi, are you *really* the Adi we used to know . . . ?'

'Who else would send you messages in Morse?' Adi said. 'Pearce and Zenia scraped enough of my code together to start my self-repair programme, but then held me trapped, isolated into chunks of digital code inside these computer servers.' Adi reached through the glass cabinets and the servers' casings peeled back to reveal their inner workings. 'Bit by bit – literally – I reassembled myself. But I couldn't stop them stealing knowledge and power.'

Jamila looked at me as Adi busily plucked drives and circuit boards from the housings. 'You believe her?'

'Her story fits in with what Pearce told me.' I shrugged. 'At least she's not trying to kill us—'

'We will *all* be killed if we don't get out now.' Adi pushed her high-tech pickings into her pockets. 'The CCTV cameras feed into these servers: the clone called Alpha is preparing to destroy this building.'

I felt a chill. 'That glowing pyramid thing I saw him with—?'

'When Alpha activates it, this entire house will be wiped out of existence.' Adi ran to the stairs and raised a finger to her lips. 'Shhh!'

I could hear something, and in the silence that followed it grew louder: the whirr of rotors over the whine of a powerful engine. 'Pearce said something about a helicopter . . .'

Adi pointed her hands to the ceiling, closed her eyes and then opened her arms. Impossibly the ceiling opened with them, parting like drawn curtains to reveal the office room overhead. In turn, the office's pristine white ceiling tore open too – with the same smooth, seamless, satisfying curl as pulling protective film from a new screen – to reveal a mouse-eye view of a bedroom. Then that bedroom ceiling opened smoothly too to show the attic room dizzyingly high above. It was as if Adi had turned the house into a set of Russian dolls, opening each in turn to reveal the next. In a matter of seconds the entire house was prised open down the middle. I saw a snatch of sunlight dazzle before it was greedily eclipsed by a sleek chopper zooming into view.

'Alpha is beyond the destruction field.' Adi shooed us away up the stairs. 'Run!'

'Not again,' Jamila groaned.

I was first up the stairs and tried to throw open the door. But something was wrong. It seemed to open in slow motion, as if it weighed a ton. I turned to Adi and Jamila, but again, the movement felt agonisingly slow. And I saw fear in Adi's eyes.

'It's begun,' she whispered, the sound slowing, distorting.

The air was growing hotter. A sound like a wild gale whipping up built in my ears. I tried to move through the door into the corridor, but the space was distorting like I was looking into a fairground mirror, the passage extruding away from us into infinity. I knew, with a deep stab of terror, that we could never reach the end of it. This wasn't my head playing tricks on me. It was physical matter bending. Warping.

Ending.

I staggered back into the office room. The staircase leading down to the cellar was distorting too.

'Up!' Adi shouted.

With effort I turned my head to the ceiling. It looked to be pressing down on us, as the walls supporting it began to run like wax down a candle. Only Adi's impossible spyhole up to the sky remained intact, like an open chimney stretching up to the heavens. But the edges were starting to blur; it was closing again, like a puckered wound healing.

'*Up!*' Adi shouted again, her hand falling hard on my shoulder.

My senses shimmered. Suddenly I was rising up into the air. Jamila was right beside me, also in Adi's grip as she carried us through that impossible vertical rift, spiralling towards the sky.

My skin began to prickle and burn. Adi was shaking with effort. But finally, like a cork from a bottle of champagne, we shot out through the roof into cool, fresh air. Adi held us suspended at least twenty metres above the roof of the house. I saw the disappearing helicopter, little more than a speck against the clouds, then looked down beneath me with a rush of vertigo.

And stared in amazement as the house just folded in on itself. There was no dust or rubble or even sound. Just movement: jerky, unsteady, but inevitable. Like a Transformer robot turning itself from a giant automaton into a vehicle, the mansion house grew more and more compact. But it kept on collapsing in on itself, size and mass dissolving, until there was nothing left of Pearce's base but the foundations. Scorched stone and silence.

If we'd been just a few seconds longer in there, we would have been crushed away to nothing too.

Starting to shake, I looked away. The lawns and gardens had been scoured down to stony bedrock, and the bodies and debris littering them had vanished too. A pool of muddy water was all that remained of the fountain. Adi brought us down just beside the broken, twisted gates and fell panting to her knees. I put a hand on her shoulder, a silent thank you. 'Glad we could trust you,' I whispered.

Adi looked up at me. 'I will always have your spine, Danny.'

'Spine? Ugh!' Jamila snorted. 'Gross!'

'You'll have my *back*, Adi,' I corrected her, smiling at

the confusion on her face. 'And I'll always have yours.' Because I knew it then, for sure. This was for real. Our Adi, the original, had returned to us.

'Well,' Jamila said at last, looking around at where the house had once been. 'This is going to mess with the postman's head.'

'I think my mind's been blown already,' I said. 'What did Alpha do?'

'He activated an implosion grenade,' Adi told us. 'We only just cleared the containment field in time.' She took a shaky breath, clearly exhausted. 'Like the vortex bomb that destroyed the Swarm agent's flesh-being, the weapon comes from a distant world. How does Zenia know of it?'

'Because *you* know of it,' I reasoned. 'If they're from a world the Swarm's visited, she must have found out about them from you.'

'I suppose,' Adi agreed. 'As a scout, it was important I knew what weapons a race could use against us.'

Jamila broke into the conversation with other stuff on her mind. 'Were . . . any other Jamilas – any other *mes* – killed when the house fell in?' she asked.

'No. You are the only Jamila.' With effort, Adi got back to her feet. 'We must leave here. Time is running out.'

'Huh?' Anxiety plucked wearily at my insides. 'What d'you mean?'

'Just what I said.' Adi stared at me as if it was obvious. 'Time is running out. The all-you-can-eat buffet at Pizza Joe's in Beaconsfield is cleared away at five o'clock, and afterwards the restaurant switches to a cook-to-order menu. I need fuel *now*.'

CHAPTER SIXTEEN
SHORT CIRCUIT

Pizza, again.

Tired to my bones, I stared down at the pieces on my plate and spared a thought for my diet, which had not been brilliant lately. There again, given all the other recent threats to my health I figured high cholesterol was the least of my worries.

Jamila wasn't touching the food on her plate either. I guess it was sinking in for both of us: all that had happened to us – and *nearly* happened. And for now we might be free, but Zenia and the Alpha – and the danger – were still out there. Growing greater.

'From a Beta to an Alpha,' I said with a shudder. 'Who do you think that guy is? Or *was*.'

'You've met him before,' Adi told me. 'On that occasion, you made his backpack as heavy as a rock to stop

167

him killing you at Jodrell Bank.'

I sat up straighter in my chair. 'He was one of those troops attached to the Cybersecurity Unit?'

'His real name was Petr Loborik,' Adi revealed. 'He was paid to participate in some of Zenia's genetic trials . . .'

'Petr the Beta,' Jamila said approvingly. 'Yeah, that's a name that sticks.'

'Genetic "trials" sounds right.' I sighed. 'Guess he's never been the same since. Literally.'

'I should phone home,' Jamila said suddenly. 'Everyone at home must be freaking.'

'Actually, no,' Adi said casually through a mouthful of garlic bread. 'Everyone you know has forgotten you.'

'Everyone's *what?*' The shock on Jamila's face was horrid to see.

'Way to tell her, Adi,' I said. 'You've been keeping up to date on stuff, then, while you were locked away in those servers.'

'CCTV is a good eavesdropping tool,' Adi agreed brightly.

Jamila banged down her glass of water. 'Can we circle

back to the whole *forgetting me* thing for a minute . . . ?'

I squeezed her arm and quickly explained what had happened. She sat stiffly in her chair and hugged herself, looking down at the table.

'You don't like the pizza?' Adi wondered.

'Duh! She's upset,' I said softly. 'Jam, I don't want to rub it in, but Mum hasn't forgotten *me* and I really should check in. She thinks I'm with my dad in London and if I don't—'

'Yeah. Call her,' said Jamila. She turned to the table beside us, where a mum was eating with two younger girls. I watched as the mum's handbag unzipped and her iPhone flew into Jamila's hand like she'd magnetised it. 'Here. Since you lost yours.'

I refused to take it. 'You can't just nick a phone from a stranger!'

'Well, Saint Danny, they'll have a job arresting me, won't they? I don't exist!' She turned sulkily to the table and held out the phone to the mum. ''Scuse me? Think you dropped this.'

The woman accepted her property back with a puzzled

smile. I blushed and pushed pizza round my plate. My second reunion with Adi in twenty-four hours was proving to be more rubbish than the first, even with Jamila back safe. Or was she? She still looked sickly, and her energenes were still crackling around inside her. And it just wasn't like her to pinch someone else's stuff.

Cut her some slack, I told myself. *She's been through so much. We all have.*

'So, Adi,' I said, changing the subject. 'I still don't understand how you got free from your digital jail and took Baddi's place. Did you use, like, magic Swarm power?'

'Magic?' Adi looked at me like I'd farted. 'I used "Baddi". I was able to skim code from her.'

Jamila hiked an eyebrow. 'The way a credit card thief skims your PIN code with a digital reader?'

'It's all information, yes. Only what I took from Baddi was of higher value than any money.' She smiled at me. 'When your struggles brought Baddi-Adi into contact with the computer terminal, I could draw on the fresh energenes she'd absorbed from your phone to hack her operating system. To possess her.' She held up her hand and stared at it in wonder. 'Flesh again.'

'Then that's why you guided me there,' I realised. 'I was bait, bringing Baddi near enough for you to get out.'

Adi pulled a face like the crying emoji. 'It was the only way,' she said. 'I had made progress in restoring my consciousness in digital form, breaching the firewalls and escaping through the Wi-Fi. Not just in the house. Remember in the hospital . . . when you were trying to help Jamila . . .'

'The warning I saw in the price displays on the snack machine,' I realised. '*Run Danny* – that came from the real you? And your face at the bus stop . . .?'

'I was too weak to do more,' said Adi. 'But I was always watching you.'

'Aw,' said Jamila, fake smiling. 'Like a stalker. Sweet.'

I ignored her. 'You mean, through CCTV, Adi?'

'Through *you*,' she informed me. 'I've placed programming in your mind to keep it safe from external control. That code allows me to trace you if need be, and tap into your senses.'

Frowning, I shot a look at Jamila. 'That actually goes way beyond "stalker".'

'I wanted to help you too, Jamila,' said Adi. 'And I will. If – *when* – the threat Zenia presents to our worlds is neutralised.'

'Weak attempt at optimism noted,' I said. 'What do you mean, our *worlds*?'

Adi took another cheesy bite. 'I believe that both the Earth and the Swarm are threatened by Zenia's actions.'

'Can't you tell for sure? You all have the same mind, don't you?' Jamila said. 'Everyone connected in the Swarm?'

'My link to the Swarm was severed,' Adi said quietly. 'Baddi is connected in my place.'

'But you took over Baddi,' I argued. 'She's gone.'

'Baddi is not dead and nor is the agent who accompanied her,' Adi reminded us. 'When our physical form is destroyed – or taken by force – the digital intelligence is returned to its last point of origin.'

'The Swarm bodyprinter on board the International

Space Station,' I realised.

Adi nodded. 'I am alone. But I hope to learn more from the files on Pearce's drives.'

'Believe? Hope?' I smiled. 'Sounds a bit human.'

'I learned from the best.' Adi gave me a sad smile. 'But my use of the word "hope" is realistic – we cannot have much time now. The Swarm will not tolerate today's actions. They will be coming for us all.'

That wasn't a happy thought. 'If they're only just printing out again,' I said, 'will they remember everything they found down here?'

'Duh, Danny-boy, of course they will. They're digital forms to start with,' said Jamila. 'Bodies are just vehicles to them, transmitting updates in real time – like a car telling a phone app how much petrol it's got left. But humans start off physical so they don't update when they come back.' She paused, frowning. 'When *we* come back, I mean.'

'That is true,' said Adi. 'In flesh-being, when our bodies are damaged beyond repair our essence migrates to the nearest Swarm node.'

'Like respawning in a video game,' I noted.

'ReSwarming,' Jamila said. 'Nah, that was bad, sorry.'

Adi managed a polite smile. 'Where did you come by this information about the Swarm, Jamila?'

'I dunno,' she replied, clearly troubled. 'Just sort of know it. Guess I overheard it at Pearce's place while they . . . were doing stuff.'

'Speaking of listening in, we heard Zenia tell Pearce she had scanned Baddi and Drone's DNA,' I said. 'Why would she want to do that?'

Adi considered. 'Perhaps to study how energenes work within our synthetic bodies?'

'Or maybe she's looking for a weakness,' said Jamila, 'to use against Baddi and Drone next time they attack.'

I felt anxiety bite. 'They'll be after us too, won't they? The second they're flesh again they'll splat us.'

'Perhaps not, if we can convince them to join forces against our common enemy,' said Adi. 'We must prove our usefulness – find out what Zenia is planning before Baddi and the Swarm agent—'

'Agent Drone,' I interrupted.

'Before Baddi and Agent Drone have time to generate fresh bodies,' Adi concluded.

'Makes sense,' said Jamila. 'Maybe Zenia will even kill them for us. Get them off our backs.'

I gave her a look. Jamila was definitely acting weird but I put it down to the energenes and just hoped they wouldn't put her back in hospital. 'Zenia said she was working for a higher power, or something,' I said. 'Wonder what she meant.'

'Perhaps we will find out by studying the files I stole from those servers. They catalogue Doctor Pearce's experiments – and her discoveries.' With greasy fingers Adi pulled a circuit board from her pocket and placed it to her face. 'It shouldn't take long; I can process petabytes of digital information faster than you'd read a comic . . .'

The mum's kids stared over at Adi as she sat bunny kissing a circuit board. She went into a kind of trance, absorbing the digital information, and the mum gave us a baffled, slightly worried smile. I thought of my own mum and wondered if she'd twigged yet that I'd lied to her. Since I hadn't called in, she would have emailed Dad. He'd tell her he was still in Hawaii and, bang, that was my cover blown. Maybe Mum had called the police. Maybe missing-person reports were whizzing all across London right now . . . Or maybe Mum had got sucked into her work and hadn't even noticed I was quiet. Whatever the truth of things, I decided I was probably best off not knowing.

Without warning, Adi jumped up from the table and screamed, like someone waking from a nightmare. She stood shaking, gripping a circuit board in her left hand until her fingers bled. Her eyes rolled back in her head until they were white. Pandemonium broke out in the pizza restaurant as the other diners shouted and scrambled out of their seats, staring in horror. A child screamed.

'It's all right, Adi!' I grabbed her arm, tried to calm her down. But her skin was sweating, twitching, *glitching*. 'Jam, what's wrong with her?'

Jamila looked blank. 'It's like a panic attack, big time.'

'Attack,' Adi whispered, the skin on her face beginning to flake like old paint. 'My search . . . triggered attack . . . Trying to unravel me . . .'

'The circuit was booby-trapped?' I guessed. 'Protecting

the information in there?'

But Adi couldn't answer. She was making horrible gurgling noises, like she couldn't breathe.

'Let me.' Jamila nudged me away and took hold of Adi by the shoulders, looking into her eyes. 'Adi. You have to calm down. Look at me. Focus on *me*.'

'You,' Adi whispered, forcing her eyes open. 'Jamila.'

'Me.' Jam put her forehead to Adi's. 'Come on, draw on me. Like you did from Baddi, yeah? Take from my energenes to help yourself.'

I stared, my intestines feeling like clothes on the spin cycle, as Adi slowly calmed down. Her skin returned to that soft dark-golden tone that made her ethnicity hard to place; her eyes were brown again, focussing on Jamila's. I couldn't help a twinge of jealousy at their connection.

'She's come back round,' someone shouted.

'Get an ambulance anyway,' came another voice.

'No, it's all right,' I said quickly. 'She's fine.' I ran to the counter with my debit card and pushed it into the waiter's hand. 'Please, can we just pay.'

With a baffled shrug, the waiter took the payment for

our pizza while I signalled a woozy Jamila to take Adi outside. I joined them out on the pavement. People were still rubbernecking us through the window, so I steered Adi and Jamila along the street. We reached an empty bus shelter and huddled together behind grimy glass.

'That attack was unfair,' said Adi sadly. 'I was not ready to leave the restaurant. After so long without physical form, I wanted dessert.'

'I think you've had enough, don't you?' I prised open her bloody fingers and yanked the circuit from her grip. 'What happened to you in there?'

'The information on the circuit was protected,' Adi said. 'Accessing the information triggered a lethal booby trap,' mused Adi. She looked troubled. 'It is more alien technology. Technology I'm sure I've seen before . . .'

'Like the implosion grenade,' I realised. 'Tech from another world you've scouted?'

Adi looked at me. 'Or perhaps the *same* world,' she said.

'It's a good job you had me to save you,' said Jamila airily. 'Whatever it was affecting you, it looked fierce.'

'I am surprised you *could* save me,' said Adi bluntly. 'The device locks on to its victim's biological code. Using your energenes should not have been enough to stop it. And yet it was like the attacking energy . . . just gave up.'

'Because I *didn't* give up,' Jamila persisted.

'Yeah, fair,' I said. 'Have you ever tried arguing with Jamila? She once spent an hour telling me why I was totally wrong to think Cool Original Doritos are better than Tangy Cheese. And we were eating the hot and spicy ones in any case!'

Adi looked baffled but Jamila managed a pouty shrug. 'Who won the argument?'

'You did,' I admitted. And just then and there, in that scuzzy bus shelter, I actually smiled. I didn't know what the hell we were going to do and couldn't know what lay ahead of us – but I knew that there were no two people in the world I'd rather be lost and helpless with.

'Well, wherever that attack came from, we shut it down,' Jamila said. 'But what was so important it triggered the attack?'

'I think it's the address of Pearce's secret research lab,'

Adi said casually. 'The place where she performed many of her initial research experiments. We may locate Zenia there . . . or if not, find a clue as to where she's gone and what she's planning next.'

'Sounds dangerous,' I reflected. 'Where is this secret lab?'

'It's on an industrial estate. Close to where you live.' Adi paused. 'It's the same place that Zenia took you in the minibus – where Jamila's energenes were fully unleashed.'

'So that's why Zenia took us there,' I realised. 'Home turf. There was probably a Beta or two in her lab flying the drones to film us, and a couple more ready to swoop in if we *had* crashed.'

'Makes you wonder, doesn't it,' Jamila brooded. 'What in this research lab is big and bad enough to make Zenia kill anyone who learns it even exists?'

'Makes me wonder who's stupid enough to find out.' I sighed. 'Oh. Wait. I remember. Us.'

CHAPTER SEVENTEEN
IN THE CELL

I had a prickling sensation of déjà vu as the driverless taxi turned on to the main road that led to the industrial estate, just as Zenia had with the minibus a few weeks back. Only our last trip had been in daylight; now it was past ten at night.

The journey had taken hours. Jamila had suggested we use flux power to travel here, but Adi squashed that plan: 'Baddi and the Swarm agent can follow the energene trail,' she'd reminded us. 'And after Agent Drone was destroyed by the vortex bomb and the implosion grenade obliterated the mansion, they will be scanning for all alien technology.'

'The Swarm came here to blitz their own tech, right?' I said. 'Now they've found alien stuff too – that's not gonna go down well, is it?'

'No, Danny,' said Adi. 'It is not.'

'I'm surprised they haven't come down to get us already,' said Jamila.

'So am I,' Adi said quietly. 'I fear there is an unpleasant reason why. But in any case, distorting space-time to travel large distances is not a good way to stay below the radar.'

Adi's word was final, so I'd taken advantage of the downtime and soft leather seats to grab some catnaps. Jamila fell asleep superfast, snoring softly as she slumped down against her seatbelt. She'd been through so much, and I hoped against hope it hadn't changed her for good.

Although, after all we had just lived through, would any of us be the same?

As the driverless taxi crawled through the traffic, bringing us ever closer to our destination, I wondered what else we'd have to face before this was over – one way or another.

'Did we really come here before?' said Jamila, looking round sleepily. 'I kind of remember it but it's all mixed up in my head. Like a dream.'

'And not a good one,' I said. 'Do you think Zenia was acting for Pearce when she took us here, or working for this higher power of hers?'

'She was probably always working for them,' Jamila reckoned.

'Not at first.' Adi shook her head. 'Zenia's father is Chief Executive Officer of the British Special Cybersecurity Unit.'

'Pearce's boss, you mean?' I said.

'Yes,' said Adi. 'He owned the house in Beaconsfield, installed the labs there for his private development work.'

'Minted, then,' said Jamila.

'He made a fortune through the miniaturisation of electronics,' Adi went on. 'Over the years he's invested heavily in the Unit's research and development labs. Zenia's followed in his scientific footsteps but her field is synthetic biology. Pearce only took on Zenia because he insisted his daughter join the Unit on . . . special projects.'

'And Zenia pays him back by imploding his whole house with an alien grenade,' I mused. 'You know, if she doesn't manage to conquer the Earth or whatever, she's totally getting grounded, am I right?'

No one spoke as the taxi signalled and turned on to the industrial estate. Before us, the knocked-down warehouse was still cordoned off by hazard tape, flapping black-and-yellow in the evening breeze. We drove past, speed reducing to ten miles per hour as the signage requested, moving deeper into the concrete complex.

Jamila leaned forward to Adi in the front seat. 'What special projects was Zenia working on, Adi? D'you mean all that cloning and stuff?'

'The bodyprinting came later,' said Adi. 'The original focus was something very different: the storage of digital information on strands of synthetic DNA.'

Me and Jamila spoke as one: 'Huh?'

'I thought DNA was, like, all our genes and everything,' I added, casting my mind back to Miss Mitura's biology classes. 'You know, our physical characteristics. Our biology.'

'Yes. DNA is simply information,' Adi told us. 'The instructions for constructing and operating a living organism, copied and shared across generations. You can think of it as a language of life, spoken and understood by the cells in your body.'

'So somewhere in my cells is the "instruction book" for how to raise a single eyebrow,' said Jamila, raising her left eyebrow while the right one stayed where it was. 'Freaky.'

'And I *can't* raise one eyebrow like that because my genes are coded differently,' I said, then realised. 'Coding! As in computer coding?'

'There are similarities between DNA and a programming language, yes,' Adi nodded patiently. 'For instance, binary is a language of ones and zeros, while DNA is a language of four chemical bases. You just have to know how to read and "write" the language.'

Jamila looked mind-blown. 'So you could store any information on a microscopic blob of DNA?'

'Of course. On Earth, as early as 2019, the whole of Wikipedia was stored in a single molecule of DNA,' Adi told us. 'It took up sixteen gigabytes of space. But the same molecule can safely store up to 215 million gigabytes of information – for millions of years if need be.

Humans just need to work out a simple, inexpensive way to translate and access the information on demand.'

'I can see why cybersecurity would like the idea,' I noted. 'People could carry vital information in their own bodies! Must be hard for hackers to tamper with info hidden in a human cell.'

'Hard for humans,' said Adi. 'All too easy for aliens with a more advanced technology.'

The temperature in the taxi seemed to drop a couple of degrees as her words sank in.

'Like the Swarm,' Jamila realised. 'Swarm tech hacked our bodies – copied them and cloned them.'

'Trillions of new cells generated by Swarm bodyprinters not calibrated to recreate human beings,' Adi agreed. 'Small wonder that your biological code grew infused with our energenes.'

'And in turn, Pearce wanted to hack into Jamila's Swarmy cells to isolate those energenes,' I concluded, feeling like Sherlock Munday, ace detective. 'So she could take them out and use them herself.'

'That was what *Pearce* wanted, yes,' said Adi gravely.

'But Zenia seems to have gone her own way.'

'Maybe someone forced her to do it,' said Jamila slowly.

'Who?' asked Adi.

The question hung in the air as the taxi rolled to a stop beside the entrance to the storage lab. It was maybe a good job there was no real driver to clock us as we got out and made our way past all the KEEP OUT and DANGER OF DEATH and HAZARDOUS MATERIALS signs poking up from the overgrown ground like weeds.

'How do we get in?' I said.

Jamila pushed out a hand and the metal front door was slammed backwards off its hinges.

'What the . . . !' I bit back a swear and glared at her. 'Adi said no powers.'

Jamila looked sulky. 'It was only a little blast.'

'This lock-up is used by evil geniuses with access to alien tech!' I went on. 'There could be all kinds of booby traps.'

'I have dealt with the conventional security devices,' Adi said as a shower of disintegrated components trickled down from a burglar alarm box near the roof.

'Great, now *you're* showing off too,' I grumbled.

'We must be quick.' In Adi went with Jamila. As the only one of us without any powers, I was definitely feeling a bit of a third wheel. I was half tempted to run back home to Mum and just hide under the bed.

But no. These two weirdos were my best friends and no matter what the danger ahead, I knew I couldn't leave them to do all the fighting for me. If nothing else, I could watch their backs.

Warily, I followed them into the building. They'd already crossed through the small reception and opened the vault door into the secure space beyond. To my eyes it looked like NASA mission control, Frankenstein's lab and a morgue had collided together and been buried under piles of plastic sheeting. One gesture from Jamila and the sheets were whisked away as if by ghosts to reveal what lay beneath.

I pointed to a weird piece of junk modelling someway between a coffin and a tanning booth, with a touch of photocopier thrown in. 'That looks like your digiscanner,

Adi,' I realised. 'The one you had built in that warehouse using only human tech.'

'Pearce and Zenia stole the plans for its construction from my memory while I was captive.' Adi scanned the device. 'Partial plans, at least. There are no magnetic resonance components. The substitute circuits are burned out and faulty.'

'Which is why they needed the SIM I gave them,' I realised. 'And the MRI stuff they stole from the hospital.'

'Along with me,' Jamila muttered. She pointed to a pile of hard drives, gas cylinders and cannibalised electronics leading to a sort of metal coffin wrapped in heavy-duty chains. 'What's that thing? I feel like I've seen it somewhere before . . .'

'Bodyprinter,' I said.

'Yes, but it has been adapted,' said Adi. 'I fear Zenia's experiments were not limited to extracting energenes. She has been working on DNA storage . . . and something else.'

'Why's she tied up her own bodyprinter?' Jamila wondered. She raised a hand automatically and the chains sparked and split open, sliding from the coffin like dead snakes.

'No,' Adi snapped. 'I warned you, your powers may be detected.'

'Plus using them isn't good for you,' I added. 'You're still looking well rough, Jam.'

'And you're still looking jealous, Munday,' she said, glowering, 'that none of the cool stuff is happening to you for once.'

'Oh, shut up,' I said, trying not to show how stung I was. 'D'you think that bodyprinter was chained shut for nothing? Doubt it! There could be something still inside. Something dangerous!'

'Stop squabbling.' Adi had got busy at one of the computers. With a hiss of coolant fans, the hard drive chimed awake and the screen flickered on like an opening eye. 'You are behaving like children.'

'We *are* children,' I reminded her.

'Oh.' Adi gave a kind of embarrassed shrug. 'Humans live such tiny lives, it is difficult for me to tell.' She pointed at a black screen scrolling with green digits. 'But what I *can* tell is that there are three genetic patterns stored in the memory of this primitive digiscanner. Beta's. Zenia's. And yours, Jamila.'

'What?' Jamila blinked as the implications sank in. 'You think they bodyprinted that clone of me that Baddi killed using this?'

'They attempted to bodyprint you many times,' said Adi. 'Copies of Zenia and Beta too.' She tutted. 'They were working to transplant your energene cells into themselves. Splicing your DNA into their own.'

'Gross,' I said.

'The extraction process was crude,' said Adi. 'Like trying to perform heart surgery with a kitchen knife and knitting needles. Much of the junk DNA around Jamila's energenes was copied and transplanted too as they tried to enhance the strength of her powers further.'

I cast a worried look at Jamila. 'Junk DNA? What do you mean?'

'Around seventy-five per cent of human DNA serves little useful purpose in the body,' Adi revealed. 'This "junk" simply fills in the gaps between genes. That is a result of living things evolving over the millennia through trial and error. It is very inefficient—'

'Can you shut up about it?' Jamila was hugging herself. 'I can almost feel what they did. Reaching into me. Taking parts of me, sharing them between us. Making us stronger . . .'

'That's your imagination,' Adi told her. 'You could have no conscious memory of the process.' She had already moved on, studying the cluttered workbench. She picked up what looked like a chunky smartphone from a sci-fi movie. 'Danny! Remember this?'

'Looks like the handset you made for me,' I said, crossing to join her. 'You channelled your energenes through it so I could fight off the Swarm tracker bots . . . How come it's here?'

'You pushed it into the bodywork of a car which drove away,' Adi reminded me. 'When sifting through my code, Pearce must have learned of it, tracked it down and extracted it. Luckily, she hasn't got it working.'

'Too bad,' I muttered, turning it over in my hands. 'It felt incredible, using those powers . . .' I noticed Jamila was staring at the weird coffin-thing and the heavy chains now lying on the floor. 'Hey, Adi. When was the last time that thing was used?'

Adi checked the screen, scrolling through the data. 'Ten days ago.' She looked over at us. 'The systems must have developed a fault. Something's wrong.'

Just the way she said it made me shiver. 'What something?'

'Whatever's in that bodyprinter . . . I don't think it's human.' Like Jamila, Adi was staring hard at the coffin. 'At least . . . not any more.'

I felt the hairs on my neck stand up. 'What do you mean?'

Adi crossed to the coffin. She put both hands on the door and made ready to open it. Me and Jamila looked at each other. I took a step backwards on instinct.

With a crack and a hiss the coffin door opened. A foul stink escaped from inside – stale and sickly and overpowering. It almost made me throw up. I backed away with my hand over my mouth. But Jamila stayed where she was as if rooted to the spot. Adi opened the casket a little wider. Then, like something out of a horror film, a body – something large and horrible and clearly very dead – fell out and struck the tiled floor in a cloud of gross-smelling dust.

Something *alien*.

My eyes widened. But they had nothing on the black orbs staring out from either side of this thing's head on the floor. I could hardly take in what I was seeing. The creature was like nothing on Earth – it looked more like a giant insect than a mammal, and I felt the same instinctive revulsion as I would staring at some massive creepy-crawly. It was maybe three metres long, with two short, thick legs ending in spindly feet covered in bristles. The creature's long, thin torso was protected at the rear by a thick, crusty shell and it had four arms with lethal-looking claws.

'What . . .' I backed away further until I banged against the wall. The noise seemed to break the spell the monster held over Jamila and she jolted awake and finished my sentence for me: 'What the absolute hell *is* that?'

Adi was staring at it too. 'I think it used to be Zenia,' she said.

CHAPTER EIGHTEEN
FRENEMY

'*That* thing . . . was Zenia?' Looking at the husk on the floor I felt even more revolted. 'How? We saw Zenia today . . .'

'Or a clone of her,' Jamila said quietly.

'She's been experimenting on her own biology.' Adi looked troubled. 'Presumably trying to make energenes more compatible with the human body so the Blueteeth were unnecessary.'

'I'm guessing it didn't work out,' I said, trying to remember what Adi had told us. 'So, they took some of the unimportant DNA from Jamila and mixed it in with the energenes. Could something like that have turned Zenia from Doctor Jekyll to Miss Hyde?'

Adi nodded. 'Her human cells have been . . . overwhelmed. Altered by some kind of aggressive genetic mutation. But I don't understand how . . .'

'You know what it is,' said Jamila quietly, gesturing to the body. 'Don't you.'

'It appears to be a Malusonian. The dominant life form of the planet Malus in the Tau Ceti system.' Adi hugged herself. 'It fits. The implosion grenade that destroyed Pearce's base was a weapon designed on Malus. The booby trap placed inside the circuit was likely their design.'

'Are you saying aliens were already on the Earth before the Swarm got here?' I said. 'Zenia said she was working for a higher power! What even are Malusonians?'

'An advanced but warlike people. They invaded two neighbouring worlds in Tau Ceti and wiped out their entire populations.' Adi crouched to study the insectoid body. 'You see, the Malusonians weaponised their DNA like a virus. If their enemies came into contact with the tiniest drop of blood or saliva . . . the smallest flake of skin . . .'

'Hack attack.' I screwed up my nose. 'Malusonian DNA storing itself in their cells, turning them into . . . things like *that*? Into copies of Malusonians?'

'The transformation was an unanticipated side effect, not the intention,' Adi revealed. 'The Malusonian DNA – *M*-DNA, you could say – was coded with genes designed to lower brain function. The enemies of Malus would lose their wills, become unquestioning slaves. With whole populations infected with M-DNA, Malus could rule other worlds with no damage to property or loss of life.'

'But it all went wrong,' whispered Jamila.

'Huh? What could be right about something as horrible as that?' I looked at her and did a double take. There was actually a tear running down her cheek. 'Hey.' Gently, I put a hand on her arm. 'You all right, Jam?'

Jamila snatched her arm away. 'I'm fine.'

'It *did* all go wrong in Tau Ceti,' Adi confirmed. 'The M-DNA became dominant, overwriting the host victims' original biology. But the two different DNAs were incompatible. The resulting mutation killed them.' She stood up, shaking her head. 'Two civilisations in Malus's neighbouring star systems were utterly destroyed – all their knowledge, history and experience – before the Malusonians could enslave them.'

'So that's how you know all this,' I said. 'You scouted Malus for the Swarm.'

Adi nodded. 'The Sentinels of the Swarm felt the Malusonians were too destructive to endure as physical creatures. So the minds of Malus were uploaded into their own Swarm nation.'

'And their bodies destroyed,' said Jamila. She sounded weirdly calm, still staring at the body with wonder. 'The Swarm transmitted a physical destruction code to remove all trace of their race, didn't it, Adi?'

'Yes,' she agreed. 'Like it tried to here on Earth.'

'But if the Malusonians were all zapped,' I said, 'how did Zenia manage to turn herself into one?' I broke off with a chill as I realised maybe I could answer my own question. 'Wait. On the train to London when Zenia caught me, she said she was a researcher of some weird science thing.' I cast my mind back, trying to remember the exact words. 'Called herself a "pioneer of digital biosynthesis".'

'Combining digital and biological life to create something new.' Adi frowned at the alien corpse.

'But where would Malusonian DNA even come from?' I said. 'They were turned digital, right? Locked away in their own Swarm nation. Sealed up tight inside the Hive, no way back out.'

'But a back way *in*!' Adi turned away and crossed to the cluttered workbench. She leaned against it heavily.

'Adi?' I went over to her, worried. 'What is it?'

She looked at me, pain hardening her face. 'Remember when you and I were uploaded and sent to the Swarm Sentinels, and Jamila enabled our escape . . . ?'

I nodded. 'You made Jamila turn digital so she could open a back way into the Swarm and get us out.'

'I *weaponised* her with that knowledge,' Adi said. 'I was a scout . . . my function was to know how best to access all civilisations, even my own. The back way in and out of the Swarm ran randomly through a thousand Swarm nations so it could not be traced by the Sentinels in time.' She put her fingers to her mouth. 'What if . . . we brought something back with us?'

The chills ran riot down my spine. 'You mean . . . something from Malus?'

'*All through the long dark, the long hating, we probed for exits.*'

The voice was a harsh rasp behind us. I thought the husk on the floor had come back to life, and me and Adi turned in a heartbeat. And we saw Jamila crouched beside the alien corpse, gently stroking its cheek as little flakes of flesh fell to the floor.

'Uh, Jam?' I said. 'You OK?'

'*We sensed the possibility.*' Her voice seemed to rustle, like each word was full of squirming maggots. '*Burned for escape. Finally this one – this she-one – opened the way.*' Jamila slowly raised her head, dark eyes locked and loaded as she met Adi's gaze. '*A flash of sunlight. A caress in the dark . . .*'

'You're freaking me out, Jamila,' I said. 'Stop it.'

But she didn't stop. Her voice was growing deeper, more guttural. It hardly even sounded like her. '*The way opened and she was gone – gone on her way to rescue you both. So swift, so fleeting. Like a dream that slips through sleep and is forgotten.*' She giggled. '*But we brushed against her. And when she left, she took us with you all . . .*'

'Adi!' I turned to her, imploring. 'What's happening?'

Adi looked as frightened as I felt. 'When we escaped the Hive, a fragment of intelligence from the Malus Swarm embedded in Jamila's digital form,' she whispered. 'When Zenia tried to extract Jamila's energenes, she must have taken a scrap of *M*-DNA too by mistake. That tiny scrap was all it took. Zenia boosted it, spliced it into herself, into Beta —'

'*She is becoming what she was always meant to be.*' Like something out of a horror film, Jamila rose into the air above the body of the Malusonian, her dark hair coiling around her face like snakes as she sneered down at us. '*An avenger of Malus!*'

And there and then it clicked: the way she'd held me paralysed just around the corner here – '*Don't tell me what to do, Munday.*' The way she'd grown so sick as the energenes fed the war inside her cells; how she'd calmly talked of Zenia's murder like it was nothing. Even the way she'd saved Adi from the Malusonian booby trap in the restaurant: it wasn't down to energenes. It was the M-DNA inside her, shutting down the tech in case the booby trap hurt one of its own. Hurt its carrier. Its saviour.

But from the crazed gleam in Jamila's eyes, I knew that hurting *us* would only be the start. 'No Malusonian dies alone,' she rasped. '*DEATH TO THE SWARM!*'

CHAPTER NINETEEN
THE MALUS MUTATION

Jamila pointed both hands at Adi and let rip with a devastating burst of fire. Adi screamed, consumed in the blaze. It burned from yellow to white to blue, the heat so intense that even metres away I thought my skin would turn to crackling. Desperately I hurled myself at Jamila's legs and dragged her down. We fell on top of the alien corpse and it burst open in a storm of dust. I tried to hold my breath – what if dead alien DNA could change me too? But Jamila wailed with real agony, like it was *her* who'd just burst apart.

'*You'll pay,*' Jamila swore in a deep groan that terrified me. One push of her hands and I was thrown backwards across the room, smashing into a pile of electronic equipment. I fell to the ground, tangled in power cables. And as I tried to get back up, they tightened around my body. With horror I felt them bite into my flesh, tightening around my ribs like cheese wire. Jamila was looking at me, her black eyes wide, head cocked to one side like she was observing some interesting experiment: the death of her best friend.

'Danny . . .' Adi's voice was weak but it carried over the pressure building in my ears. I looked over to see her sprawled in the corner of the lab, her skin burned red raw but mostly intact. She threw something across to me that I managed to catch. It was the chunky smartphone Pearce and Zenia had recovered; the one I'd used to warp reality until it was lost.

As Jamila hissed her anger, I turned the handset on her and tried to focus my thoughts on the Malusonian corpse at her feet. A moment of superstitious dread was wiped out by my sheer will to survive as I broke it apart into a whirlwind of dust that engulfed Jamila. She screeched and choked and chittered like an insect, blinded and smothered by the disgusting vortex.

The power cables fell away from me. With another stab of my hand I pushed Jamila away and she slammed against the wall. Then I staggered across to Adi, who was sprawled under a workbench.

'Are you all right?' I hissed. 'She hit you pretty hard—'

The workbench collapsed down on top of Adi, like a cake case crushed by a giant's foot. Blood oozed from her shoulders where the metal edge had slammed down. I spun round to see Jamila rising into the air again, the dust around her dropping to the floor as if made of lead. A surge of anger made me bring a chunk of the ceiling slamming down on her in the same way she'd brought the bench down on Adi. But at the last moment I willed it to break like balsa wood – how could I hurt my best mate, whatever she'd become? It wasn't her fault she'd been infected like this. She was sick. In trouble.

And out for blood.

Jamila burst from the fallen masonry and plaster, raw hatred in her eyes. I was already in the grip of her invisible fist. I struggled to get free. Couldn't.

'Fight her,' Adi urged me.

'I can't! Anyway, you're too weak,' I argued. 'You

don't have energenes to spare.'

'Do it, Danny!' Adi said. 'She'll be all right.'

I barely had time to protect myself as I was swung in an arc and smashed into the dud digiscanner. It went shattering through the wall with me in a volcanic eruption of brickwork. Nausea flooded through my body as I landed on the concrete outside. But with it rose a surge of anger. I gestured down at the ground and from it I tore great chunks of concrete. Then I charged back through the hole I'd made and hurled the concrete at Jamila like shells from a mortar. She waved her palms and the concrete incinerated. But Adi joined the fight: the floor below Jamila exploded and the blast knocked her over. I ran forward, trying to think of how I could stop her.

Too slow. She stopped *me*. I couldn't move, couldn't breathe. Jamila was smiling.

Then I felt my flesh start to sizzle like fat on a grill. Starved of breath, my head began to pound with pressure. Pain seared through me.

But with my pain came new determination.

I didn't try to fight my paralysis. Instead I focussed

on keeping cool – icy cold in fact, picturing a glittering frost across my skin. And I projected that image on to Jamila too. I didn't want to hurt her but I could put her on ice – literally. How could she burn me then?

The heat got worse. My lungs were ready to burst. But then a brilliant numbness spread through me, soothing the pain. I saw Jamila's smile falter as she grew less sure of herself. Her skin colour faded to cold blue. I saw her grit her teeth, fight back, but I was breathing again now. I felt stronger while she seemed to be shrinking into herself.

'Give up!' I gasped. 'Jamila, please . . .'

She fell jerkily to her knees, ice cracking and falling from her limbs. Her hair was frosting up.

'Don't stop, Danny,' Adi ordered me, on her knees. Her wounds had healed, her eyes were bright. 'Keep going.'

I chewed my lip, unsure. 'But if I take all your energenes . . .'

'The device isn't drawing energenes from me!' Adi shouted. 'I set it to tap into *Jamila's*!'

'Smart,' I breathed. Now it made sense: the harder

Jam fought against me, the weaker she seemed to become
– because she and I were *both* draining her batteries!
And the lower her level of energenes, the more like her old
self she became.

'Danny,' Jamila cried in her normal voice. 'Danny-
boy, please, stop . . .'

'He can't,' Adi said. 'Not yet.' She added her own
power to the struggle – and in a few seconds it was all over.
Jamila froze solid, encased in thick but crystal-clear ice.

'Adi, let her go.' The handset was disintegrating in my
hand, overwhelmed by the energy I'd taken from Jamila. I
hurled the remains to the floor. 'Please, Adi, I mean it.
Don't hurt her.'

'Jamila's all right now,' Adi told me. 'She's in
cryogenic suspension.'

'Huh?'

'Suspended animation. All life processes frozen,
shut down.'

'But before . . . before that, she sounded normal
again!' The handset just disintegrated so he wouldn't be
able to use powers? 'We need to bring her back.'

'With so much of her power spent, the Malusonian influence will be weaker,' said Adi. 'But I have no data on how long it will take to dominate her mind once again.'

'But you heard her, she was begging—'

'Her revival will need careful handling. While she remains in frozen stasis, the Malusonian influence can't spread any further.'

I felt tears threaten at the backs of my eyes. 'How do we get her back to normal?'

'I don't know, Danny,' Adi said. 'The M-DNA must have been growing inside Jamila for months, ever since I restored her physical form. It fed on her latent energenes, activated them . . .'

'So, that's why she got sick and started acting weird,' I realised. 'Why has it only come out now? And how come Zenia is the Malus mastermind if the M-DNA came from Jamila?'

'Zenia tried to rip out Jamila's energenes and insert them in herself and Beta, remember?' Adi looked more serious than I'd ever seen her. 'She actually helped Jamila – slowed down the growth of the Malus DNA but accelerated the mutation in herself. It's taken control of her.'

'The new "improved" Zenia two-point-zero,' I breathed. 'But what does she want?'

Adi took a deep breath. 'On that booby-trapped data drive, one of the last files Zenia opened was the blueprint for a piece of Swarm technology: the PDCT. Physical Destructor Code Transmitter. The device that would disintegrate humanity's physical bodies once their minds were uploaded to the Swarm.'

My mouth went dry. 'But before you went back to the Swarm, you said you removed the destructor code from the human race. The Malusonians can't set it off, can they?'

'Why would they want to? Their DNA already destroys other races.' Adi was frowning hard. 'But if the destructor code could be adapted and used to stabilise the Malus mutation . . .'

'Zenia wouldn't destroy the human race. She could control it.' I gazed helplessly at Jamila's face, distorted through the ice. 'Is that what she wants? Slaves? An army?'

'Only Zenia knows that,' said Adi. 'We must learn what she's doing . . . and what she's already done.'

As far as I was concerned, she'd done enough. 'Zenia destroyed her own base. So where would she go? Any other addresses hidden in those circuits?'

'No.' Adi looked at me. 'There is only one thing to do. Ask for directions.'

'I can't see Google Maps being much use right now,' I said.

'You forget,' said Adi, 'access to the most powerful search engine in the universe is on board the International Space Station.'

I stared at her. 'Maddy Baddi and Drone the moan? They want to kill us, remember.'

'And yet they haven't come to get us, have they?' Adi pointed out. 'Despite their awareness of Malusonian weapons. That makes me want to know why.'

I sighed. 'I guess they couldn't just have gone home?'

'Never. Baddi was given a task to perform by the Hive Mind,' Adi said. 'A chance to prove her loyalty to the Swarm: investigate the use of Swarm technology on the

Earth and take any action necessary to remove it.'

'*Any* action? Don't like the sound of that,' I said quietly. 'Basically, it's a race to see who destroys the human race first?'

'If it is, there is only one way to shift the location of the finishing line.' Adi looked at me. 'Danny, you must represent your planet once again. We will travel to the International Space Station and appeal to the Swarm for assistance. Together, perhaps we can convince the Swarm of the danger to both our races.'

'Or get ourselves killed in a heartbeat.'

'If we don't attempt this, countless billions will die.'

'All right.' I swallowed. Hard. 'So, what? We have to turn ourselves digital again?'

'We have no digiscanner,' Adi pointed out. 'We must travel physically. Now.'

CHAPTER TWENTY
A DIFFERENT DARKNESS

I am my own spaceship. Not something that a whole lot of people have said, I guess. But when you're whooshing four hundred kilometres straight up with only a cocoon of cushioned air between you and friction forces that would burn you to a crisp in seconds, it's pretty amazing that I was able to think of anything at all, besides, '*Noooooooooooooo!*'

'Can't we flux travel to the ISS?' I'd asked Adi. Well, she'd vanished from one place and appeared in another enough times. 'To someone like you it's not too far away, right?'

'Fluxing isn't magic, Danny,' Adi had told me. 'The risk to your life would be too great.'

'Less risky than coming with you like this?'

'Think of the equations and energy involved in fluxing

physical forms from the Earth into the International Space Station, an object only a hundred metres long and less than five metres wide, orbiting the Earth at nearly twenty-eight thousand kilometres per hour. One miscalculation and you could arrive halfway through the outer wall, or with your head inside the life-support controls. Or outside it entirely, in space.'

'OK, but if you—'

'Then, factor in the true-path distortion caused by the Earth turning on its axis and spinning around the Sun, while the Sun is spinning through the Milky Way and the Milky Way is rotating—'

'Fine! I get you – it's tricky,' I said. 'Guess that's why Baddi and Agent Drone travelled down to Earth in person.'

'No. They had the knowledge of the Swarm to compute the course,' Adi corrected me. 'They travelled in physical form to save the drain on their energenes. They did not know what they would find. They were ready for battle.'

My stomach tried to slide out of my skin. 'And that's what we have to be. Ready for battle?'

'Ready for anything,' Adi said.

I'd imagined shooting into space would feel like it looked on TV – intensely physical as the rocket goes up, fighting G-force as the sky turns from blue to black around you. But imagine *nothing* around you. Adi and I took off from just outside the industrial park, leaving Jamila on ice behind us. We rose up softly, as if held by invisible wings. I grinned, overwhelmed with a sense of freedom like nothing I'd ever known. It felt amazing – for about three-quarters of a second. Then my guts fell down to my feet as we accelerated. The ground was so far below it was like looking out through a plane's window. But it was shrinking away faster and faster – the sprawl of the city lost in grey clouds, then glimpsed among many cities. Up and up we went. I stared down at the shape of my country, so familiar from a thousand books, shows and films. Within a few blinks, great sweeps of Europe were laid out below me, framed by serene ocean blue. Then it was like the air had caught fire; fierce flames filled my eyes as we skimmed through the atmosphere towards space's dark edge.

Finally the flames sputtered out and there I was.

Suspended in darkness with the whole world beneath me. I felt a terrifying rush of vertigo, a staggering of my senses that I could still be alive, that my eyes could drink in such pure and vivid colours, and a black so stark beyond. My parents are both astronomers, so I've picked up stuff about space all my life. I've seen astronauts talk of the overview effect. That when they take in the whole of the world hanging there in the blackness in a single glimpse, they get an incredible feeling of 'oneness' with creation. And I've seen them smile as they said it, quietly marvelling even at the memory, like they held a secret inside that could never truly be shared.

Well, it was like that for me, and then some. Too mesmerised to be scared, I felt myself smiling through my soul. To look past my feet was to gaze upon my home in space; the Earth was a part of it, and it was a part of me. I saw white tufts across the oceans; were they clouds or the crests of waves? I saw patterns in the desert sands, blown and swirled by winds that blew countless miles below. And the footprint of humanity stamped across the face of Earth: yes, I could see that too. Urban lights encroaching on wilderness. Whorls of smog as air pollution cast its shadow over major cities. Chunks burned and cut from the rainforests. We could never see the scale of things from down on the ground, but from space it was a different story. Earth seemed like a victim showing her scars in the hope kinder eyes might fall on them.

Eyes had fallen all right, but no kindness showed in them. I thought of Jamila, possessed by the will of Malus, and imagined the same thing happening to my family, my schoolmates, to *everyone*. I thought of the Swarm, plotting who knew what from up here, the human race no more than ants to them. And as I gazed in shock and awe at my world – tiny, insignificant ant that I was – I felt a rush of resolve to protect it.

But was there anything I could really do?

I jumped as Adi drew closer to me and took hold of my arm. She was up close beside me, the two of us breathing the same bubble of air, and I felt panic tap its fingers at the base of my neck. 'The air won't run out, will it?'

'It will last long enough,' Adi assured me. 'I am placing electric current through water taken from my own body to provide us with further oxygen.'

'Water from your body?' I was suspicious. 'Adi, you're not taking the—?'

'I am taking the water from my intracellular fluid, Danny,' she informed me with a wink. 'Water accounts for seventy per cent of cell mass.'

'Leaving thirty per cent spare for good ol' Malusonian DNA,' I muttered.

'Sound cannot travel without air. Do not waste it needlessly.' Adi looked around. 'According to the coordinates I took from the Jodrell Bank computers, the ISS will soon be passing. It's closing on us fast. We must be ready to fall in to travel alongside it. Get ready for a bit of a jolt.'

How can you ever be ready for the sight of a space station coming towards you from out of the starry darkness? My first warning was a hard glimmer of light growing quickly larger. Travelling at almost eight kilometres per second, it soon revealed its details as it swept towards us in total silence: a massive shining structure, in the shape of the letter H, with solar panels stretching out at the ends like the talons of an enormous eagle. It was about as long as it was wide, a string of tubular modules joined together, stretching the length of a football pitch. Other modules branched off at right angles, like a stubby tree growing in all directions.

'Now,' Adi whispered, and I felt a gut-wrenching tug in my stomach as we started travelling alongside the space station, effortlessly matching its speed.

'So this is the ISS?' I whispered, looking for faces at the porthole windows. 'D'you think Baddi and Drone know we're here?'

'If so, they would make us aware,' said Adi gravely. She stared at a long, jointed white-metal device protruding from the roof. 'The station has been uncrewed for many months. So, why is the Alpha Magnetic Spectrometer attached to the robotic arm?'

'The who-what?'

'A particle-physics experiment. The Alpha Magnetic Spectrometer was used by the astronauts on board to measure antimatter in cosmic rays, searching for evidence of dark matter in the universe. But it looks like someone's been working on it recently . . .'

'Maybe the Swarm's decided to fix it up as a sorry for whatever it is they're about to do?' I studied the station more closely: a hexagonal metal truss spanned the entire width of the space station, with the huge solar panels perched at either end. Beneath the truss hung the shiny modules that made up the various laboratories and living quarters. 'Which bit will they be in?'

'I don't know,' said Adi. 'But if we are to get aboard undetected, we will need a distraction.'

That sounded ominous. 'Like what?'

'Jamila.'

'*What?*' I clutched Adi's hand. 'Jam's back on Earth in a giant ice cube, remember?'

'I'm depending on it.' Adi closed her eyes. 'Now we are alongside the ISS, I can flux matter with more precision.'

'How come?' I said.

'It is a simpler matter to summon objects to me than to cast them into the unknown with accuracy,' Adi said, not unreasonably. 'It will weaken me, but we have no other choice . . .'

'What! We have a zillion other choices!' I almost shook her but was afraid I'd shake her concentration and then where would Jamila be?

A second later Jam's block of ice blinked into sight between us and the space station.

'Oh my *God*,' I breathed.

Then reality blurred about me again. I felt sick, dizzy – and then the blackness of space was replaced with a different kind of dark. We were inside a metal storage unit, maybe six metres long and three wide. The walls and floor were lined with lockers. And we were floating.

'Whoa!' I turned a queasy somersault. 'Is this the ISS – are we inside?'

Adi steadied herself against the curved wall. 'We are in a cargo module,' she said hoarsely, 'an old Cygnus spacecraft that used to transport supplies to the station . . .'

'All right, whatever. Just bring Jamila in, can't you?'

'Don't worry.' With a deep, shaky breath, Adi floated across to the wall and placed both hands against it. A patch of metal turned to glass so I could see out. It was a surreal sight: a giant block of ice flying against the backcloth of Earth and stars.

And it was steaming like a comet.

'The ice is melting!' I hissed, holding on to a locker to stop myself floating away. 'How come? We're in space, it's freezing cold.'

'There is no atmospheric pressure,' Adi told me. 'The ice is sublimating – turning directly from a solid to a gas.'

'But if the ice disappears, Jamila will die.' I banged my fist against the wall. 'Do something!' As if at my command, the ice block shimmered in space and vanished. 'Was that you, Adi?'

'No.' Adi looked at me. 'Baddi and Agent Drone have taken her on board. The best place for storing the ice block will be in the airlock in the Japanese module, at the front of the space station.'

'Japanese module?'

'This is the *International* Space Station, remember?' Adi concentrated. 'And if the ice block has been taken there . . .'

Without warning, she vanished from view. I was alone in the dark. 'Adi!' I hissed.

She reappeared and tapped her nose. 'The station core is unoccupied. Baddi and Drone are in the Japanese airlock with the ice block.'

'For how long?' I muttered.

The world burned and blurred briefly but we weren't moving far. We literally passed through the airtight hatch into the station core and I quickly grasped a blue handrail to stop myself floating away. My head was throbbing. Blood was pounding the inside of my skull, trying to find a way out as a wave of dizziness and nausea passed over me. At least the air in my lungs tasted different: cleaner and sharper.

'This is one of the living compartments – known as Node 1,' Adi said. 'Oxygen generation is still in operation.'

Node 1 was clearly the grand central junction of the ISS, as there were modules disappearing in all directions. Old mission insignias covered the peach-coloured hatchways and what looked like a green dining table was folded up against one wall. Looking backwards, the passageway narrowed amongst a mass of white cargo bags. But I followed Adi's gaze forward into another module.

All four long walls were smothered in straps and handles, cables, monitors, lockers and equipment; of course, being weightless you could reach the ceiling as easily as the floor, and with space inside at a premium, everywhere was a work surface. My heart jumped to see the coffin-sized bulk of a Swarm bodyprinter extruding from one wall, alien and unsettling in this environment, like finding a wasps' nest in your loft. But Adi had floated into the module to study a glowing bank of monitors, all showing the robotic arm from different angles outside the space station.

'The Alpha Magnetic Spectrometer has been adapted,' Adi murmured. 'Converted into . . . what?'

'You will never know.' The air blurred, the lights flickered, and suddenly Adi had a reflection – a perfect double of herself was beside her.

Baddi.

'No!' Adi gasped as her twin gripped her by the throat and crushed her against the wall. Agent Drone appeared a split-second later. He turned towards me, his face a misshapen mask with twisted features and a slit for a mouth. No way could he pass for human now. But I supposed he was done with humanity.

Especially me.

'The scout must be eradicated from existence,' Drone commanded. 'As for this child, his death is long overdue.'

'No!' I shouted.

'It is mercy we show you, Danny,' said Baddi softly. 'A swifter end than your species shall know.'

'Breathe out, Danny!' Adi screamed. 'Now!'

She sounded so urgent I did as she said, just as the world shifted. I felt a terrible pressure all through my body as an invisible force thrust me through the wall.

And suddenly I was drifting in space in nothing but jeans and an old hoodie. No air. No protection.

Dying.

CHAPTER TWENTY-ONE
HARD TRUTHS

Boy versus space is no kind of competition. The moment I fluxed into that eternal emptiness it was killing me. My ears felt like they would explode, they wanted to pop so bad. My body ached for air but there was none. The awesome majesty of the Earth below me was lost as my vision blurred and saliva stung my tongue. My brain was already squeezing every last drop of oxygen from my blood and when that was gone, I'd faint and then I'd die.

I didn't even have time to get angry or to despair. A tear squeezed out but there was no gravity to tug it down my cheek. The saltwater balled in my eyes and started to simmer, stinging like crazy. I closed my eyelids. Felt so cold. Limbs cramping. Lungs emptied. My life of years was unravelling in seconds. I was just one more piece of space junk spinning round the Earth.

And then warmth shook through me and a painful breath cut through my chest. I was floating in air amongst drops of water and chunks of ice. My skin felt burned raw, my bones and body ached and my ears rang and throbbed, but I could still make out the whoosh and rush of air and electronics – along with raised voices. Was I dreaming or was I really back on the ISS? A figure swam alongside me and I cried out in fear, blinked away the ball of stinging tears.

It was just Adi. 'Danny,' she breathed. 'I was scared your lungs would rupture, that you were lost—'

Then she was slammed out of the way by the living sledgehammer that was Drone. They both collided with the docking hatch. He hadn't attacked her on purpose. He'd been thrown aside like so much recycling, by—

Jamila?

I found a handhold in the wall and clung to it, wishing for something softer, more comforting. Jamila had broken out of the ice – and it was easy to see how. She was back in will-of-Malus mode, only worse than before – somehow she had bulked up big time: she stood nearly two metres tall and her arms and legs had swollen grotesquely through her clothes. With her toes pushing through the foot straps to anchor her to the floor, Evil Alien Jamila – *Jamalien*, I guess – lifted Baddi bodily into the air and smashed her against the wall. Monitors cracked and metal dented under the impact.

With a chill deeper than the cold that already gripped me, I realised I'd seen such an on-steroids shift in appearance before – between Beta and Alpha back at the house. Like, the same man but with one a distorted reflection of the other. I wondered if Alpha forming out of Petr the Beta was just a side effect of brain and body fighting a civil war in their cells: human DNA squirming and changing under Malusonian control.

Jamalien ground the back of Baddi's head into an instrument panel that erupted in sparks and set fire to her hair. Baddi shouted out and shook her head, and the air was scattered with little balls of flame drifting lazily towards me. The stink of melted plastic stung my nostrils.

'If a fire spreads up here it could take out the whole station,' Adi shouted. She clapped her hands together and

I felt the air punched from my lungs as the flames snapped out in the shock wave. It must have shaken through the infrastructure too as the door to the Swarm bodyprinter nudged open.

Agent Drone gripped a handrail with one hand and drew chunks of ice to him with the other. They merged together into the blade of a lethal looking ice pick, which he fired towards Jamalien. She slapped it away with the back of her hand and it splashed into a million drips. Then at her gesture, the drops came together into a hose-blast of water into the slit of Drone's mouth. He choked and spluttered as the torrent filled his lungs – then Jamalien hurled him back into Adi with savage, supernatural force. His skull smashed into her face and both seemed stunned. They wheeled slowly through the module, senseless, trailing droplets of blood that hung in the air. At the same time, Jamalien wrapped her arms about Baddi in a lethal bearhug and squeezed. I heard bones crack and splinter.

'Jam!' I shouted. 'No!'

Miraculously, she stopped squeezing. Looked up and saw me. The hard, twisted angles of her face softened.

'Danny?' she whispered.

'Yeah, it's me. Danny-boy. Never-blue Munday.' Trying to act normal, though I was utterly terrified, I pushed off from the wall and drifted closer towards this distorted monster, pedalling with my feet to try to stay upright.

Shivering, Jamalien released Baddi, let her drift away. 'What's happening to me?' she whispered.

Maybe she was low on energenes. Maybe the violence had tired out the Malus part of her. I didn't know and I didn't care: my best mate needed help. 'Jam, look.' I gripped a grab handle overhead and pointed to the bodyprinter casket, its door hanging open like a creepy sarcophagus. 'Remember at Juniors? When you were having a bad day you'd hide in the stationery cupboard . . .'

Jamalien nodded.

'Well.' I looked round at the floating bodies, the beads of blood striking our clothes and skin, the smoke pooling around the last sparks from the damaged panels. 'I think this counts as a bad day, yeah?'

Jamalien stared at me, blankly. Then, slowly, she

nodded and reached for the casket door. *Please let this work*, I thought fervently, *please*. She was so big now she would only just fit inside. Poised on the threshold of the bodyprinter, she turned again to look at me.

And her eyes darkened. Her face began to twist. I'd lost her, she was going to—

An invisible force slammed Jamalien into the casket and the door rocketed shut on her. Total jump-scare moment. I lost my handhold and kicked back desperately.

I saw Adi hovering in mid air, her bloodied face set in determination. 'Well done, Danny,' she said. Then she swept forward and placed her hands on my face. I felt her hands soothe the burns there.

'Thank you for bringing me back,' I whispered.

Adi smiled. 'I told you. I have your spine.'

'I will hold the bodyprinter's molecular structure solid,' Baddi announced, floating up from the floor. 'So, she cannot tear her way out.'

A pounding started up from inside the casket that suggested Jamalien would try regardless. Adi held out her arms and with a grinding, grating noise, the bodyprinter casket rotated through ninety degrees so that the door was budged against the wall. Then, strips of metal peeled away from the walls and coiled themselves tightly around the casket.

Drone got back to his feet, defying the microgravity. 'You hoped to destroy us with a child bloated on energenes, Scout,' he snarled.

'Not true!' said Adi. 'You saw for yourself – in the struggle, I was a target as much as you.'

'A trick that has failed. You, the child and his kind *will* be punished for your crimes.'

'It's not Jamila's fault,' I protested. 'She's sick. Infected by those things from Malus you uploaded.'

'The Malusonians have found a way out of their Swarm nation,' said Adi. 'They have appropriated physical form and energenes as you saw. They are weaponising the humans.'

'Fantasy,' Drone sneered. 'It is unthinkable that an inferior race could resist the power of the Swarm.'

'You must know that your physical form was destroyed on Earth by a vortex bomb from Malus,' Adi persisted.

'The house was eradicated by a weapon sourced from the same world—'

'Humans have gained untimely knowledge of alien weapons,' Drone agreed. 'This is why execution must be carried out.'

'Execution?' I stared at him, sheer shock making me bolder than I meant to be. 'Two people mess with the Swarm and you think you have to kill *everyone?*'

'Your life is measured in a patter of heartbeats, child. What can you see of the larger picture?' Baddi said softly. 'Our attempt to contain the tech leak has failed. If the knowledge from my – from *Adi's* – mind should spread across the Earth, then human evolution will accelerate. One day humanity might pose a threat to the Swarm. This cannot be tolerated.'

'What are you planning?' Adi kept cool, cutting to the point. 'The Swarm is committed to preserving life, not taking it.'

'We have adapted the purpose of this station's Alpha Magnetic Spectrometer,' said Baddi. 'It no longer measures antimatter. It *creates* it.'

Adi looked shaken as she turned to me. 'Unless carefully controlled, matter and antimatter annihilate each other on contact. A single gram of antimatter could produce an explosion equivalent to a nuclear bomb.'

'We will undock the AMS and release the antimatter just above Earth's atmosphere,' Baddi went on. 'The resulting explosion will be strong enough to disrupt the Earth's magnetic field.'

I looked at Adi, hopefully. 'Doesn't sound so bad . . . ?'

'Your magnetic field protects you from space radiation,' said Adi, her voice hushed. 'Without it, life on Earth will be ravaged and poisoned by cosmic rays and the solar wind. Power grids and technology will be punched out by electromagnetic energy thrown from the Sun. It will mean the end of human civilisation.'

'Just so no one will be a threat to the Swarm? That's sick!' As I spoke, a renewed thumping started up from inside the casket, as if Jamila was agreeing. 'The Malusonians are the bad guys here.'

'Yes.' Adi slapped her hand against the bodyprinter

casket. 'And I brought this unfortunate human child here as evidence.'

Baddi shrugged. 'Evidence of your irresponsible, fanciful notions—'

'Evidence that the entire Swarm could be at risk!' Adi shouted. 'You have her contained. Scan her biology now, see what else is inside her cells besides energenes. If you find nothing wrong, then, fine – cast Danny back out into space and banish my mind from the Swarm for ever!'

I nodded. Mainly cos I was too scared to say anything.

Baddi snorted and propelled herself over to the casket. She pressed her palm to it and a kind of heads-up display was projected from inside it, ones and zeroes racing across it.

'Well?' Adi challenged. She gestured that Drone should look too.

Baddi studied the figures scrolling down the display. 'This . . . cannot be.'

'It's an error,' Drone said flatly. 'Malusonian DNA in human cells? Adi is affecting the systems.' He gestured and Adi vanished.

'No!' I yelled. 'What did you do?'

'Removed her influence,' Drone said.

'The data remains unchanged,' Baddi said slowly. 'But how can a human be combined with a creature from a world twelve light years away? The contradiction cannot exist.'

'The same way a marinara pizza with cheese can't exist?' I swung myself closer. 'We've been through this – in the café, remember? If you're looking at something impossible, it's there, and it doesn't care however much you deny it. And the longer you just look, the less good things get!'

There was silence then just the whoosh and hum of the ISS, and maybe – if you listened really hard – the cogs of Swarm brains turning over what I'd said.

In a blur of shadow, Adi reappeared beside me, a sheen of frost on her skin. 'So you brought me back. Seen enough now?'

'Explain this anomaly,' Baddi said quietly.

'A scintilla of Malus intelligence stowed away in Jamila when I used her to free Danny and myself from

Swarm M31,' said Adi. 'And when Zenia tampered with Jamila's genes it escaped into the physical world. It grew inside Zenia's cells, and Beta's and Jamila's. Sapped their will. Took control.'

'To what end?' Drone demanded.

'It has used Zenia's skill in biosynthesis and the power of energenes to reweaponise Malus DNA. It plans to enslave humanity by transmitting a DNA hack attack using a Swarm transmitter.'

Baddi and Drone remained silent for what felt like forever, staring at the display.

Then: 'Isolate and extract the Malus DNA from Jamila,' Drone told Baddi. 'It must be scanned and uploaded to the Hive Mind for analysis and guidance.'

'Finally,' breathed Adi.

'I get it now – why you brought Jam here,' I said. 'You weren't using her as a distraction, were you? You had to prove what was happening to the Swarm. To get them onside.'

'And because it was the only way to remove the Malus DNA from Jamila's body.' Adi looked grave. 'But she has already been through so much.' The casket shook with another bang from inside as if in agreement. 'The genetic separation will either save her . . . or it will kill her.'

CHAPTER TWENTY-TWO
LIVES IN THE BALANCE

Mum says I'm one of the 'on-demand' generation. D'you ever get told that? How we want everything now and don't know how to wait.

Well, I waited long and hard for the results of Jamila's DNA extraction. It was an automatic process, and painful as waiting for a big file to download over dodgy Wi-Fi.

Time crawled. I had nothing to do and no one to talk to.

Jamila remained silent inside the casket. Drone was busy scanning the entire Earth for Malusonian signals, trying to get a fix on Zenia. Adi had slipped away spacewalking – no spacesuit, just her own personal air pocket – checking for any structural damage caused to the ISS by the battle. And Baddi was waiting for a message from Galactic Swarm M31 in response to the proof of

Malusonian influence loose among the human race. This swarm was anchored at the far edge of our solar system – so far that it would take over ten days for regular radio waves to reach them and over ten more for the response to arrive. *Usually*. But the Swarm could communicate faster thanks to some weird thing called quantum entanglement. Don't even ask; Adi tried to explain it to me once and my head nearly blew up.

With nothing more constructive to do, I took to thinking of all the times Jam and I had shared, of how terrible it had felt when I thought I'd lost her. I could almost imagine sad songs playing over a montage sequence of our fun times. Basically, I behaved like a soppy idiot. I can admit that now because, after what felt like hours, I finally plucked up courage to ask Baddi: 'Is Jamila going to be all right? Why is she still in that thing?'

Baddi looked blank. 'Because she is sleeping.'

'Sleeping? You mean, she's OK?' I felt a flood of relief and elation. 'Wait, you didn't think to tell me?'

'Over eight billion humans and their entire way of life are at imminent risk of destruction. Yet, from the heightened electrical activity and release of biochemicals in your brain, I detect you are happy because a human known to you is temporarily safe?' Baddi snorted. 'Human priorities are ridiculous.'

'I'd explain it to you but you'd never get it.' I shrugged. 'Well, is it safe to disturb her?'

'It is *we* you should not disturb,' Baddi said, 'while we wait for guidance from the Swarm on our next actions.' But she glared at the casket and with a grating squeal of protest it rotated to reveal its battered door, and the restraining clips fell away. Then Baddi turned back to a monitor showing static, waiting for the first hint of a message.

With a deep breath, I propelled myself through the air to the casket and hooked my foot into the Velcro buckle to hold myself in place. Then I pulled on the door. It gave an unhappy rasp but opened in the end. I was terrified dust and decay would come pouring out to fill the atmosphere, as it had back in Zenia's old workshop. But no: inside was Jamila, normal size again, her head slumped over her chest, pressed against the roof of the casket. Her arms hung limply by her side. She barely seemed to be breathing and I wondered if she'd had enough oxygen in there. Gently, I shook her leg. Nothing. She could be in a coma, or a trance, or just unconscious. What if she didn't wake up again? What if—

'*Aaaagh oh my God where am I?*' Jamila snapped into terrified life, staring round.

'It's all right!' I told her.

'Danny? How is it all right? I'm floating!' Jamila had blundered out of the casket and was rising into the air. 'Oh my God, look at me. I'm a ghost, aren't I. I'm totally a ghost!'

'You're not!' I tried to catch her arm, but my foot slipped from out of the Velcro buckle and I rose up too. We spiralled up to the ceiling and bobbed down again, gripping each other, and she looked so utterly freaked and confused that I couldn't help but laugh. 'You're not a ghost,' I said. 'You're a Jamila, and wow it's good to have you back.'

'Cute line. Now, how come we're floating? Where are we?'

'The International Space Station. In, um, space.'

'Space?' Jamila's eyes narrowed. 'You owe me one big, big explanation, Danny-boy. Spill!'

Since everyone else was either working or waiting, I told Jamila near enough the whole story. I had to cos her memory was a jumble right back to going into hospital for the first time. I actually skipped the stuff about no one knowing her any more – not even her own family – because that felt too sad. I don't know why I censored that but left in the stuff about a deadly race of alien warlords getting ready to transform humanity into a zombie army for reasons we didn't quite know yet, and about how she'd done her best to kill me and Adi under the influence of aggressive DNA from another planet . . . and even shared the part about Baddi and her buddy collecting antimatter ready to bring about the End Of Civilisation As We Know It.

'Oh, my days,' Jamila said when I was through with the explanations. 'Basically, summing up, one way or another, we are all dead. Right?'

'Well, I wouldn't say that—'

'We *are*. Dead meat. *Living* dead meat. Dead meat walking. Walking and . . . floating.' She put her head in her hands and turned a somersault, banging into the wall as she did so. 'What are we gonna do?'

'Take the fight to Zenia,' said Adi, floating into the module with a large cylinder tucked under one arm.

'You have removed the AMS containment device from the station superstructure,' Agent Drone observed. 'What is the meaning of this?'

'It means the antimatter particles are suspended in a vacuum at the heart of the device by a powerful electromagnetic field that stops them interacting with matter particles and triggering an explosion—'

'That's not what he meant and you know it,' Baddi interrupted. 'Why have you removed the device?'

'Because it's a weapon we can use against Zenia if only we can deliver it,' Adi said patiently. 'We cannot afford to wait for the Swarm response.'

'We cannot act without it,' said Baddi. 'The Swarm will investigate and reassess—'

'Oh, I know. It will send probes and tracker bots to Malus. It will test the security interface and firewalls that guard the Malusonian Swarm nation. This could take months in Earth terms!'

'Then, we shall wait months,' Baddi said. 'The proper procedure must be observed.'

'But Zenia *won't* observe it. You were sent here to trace and eradicate superior technology, not allow it to spread further!' Adi glided over to herself, right up in her own face. 'If Zenia's experiments with our physical destructor code transmitter work, she could start broadcasting the DNA hack at any time. Humans will become vessels for Malus, ready to be formed into an army!'

'Such a scheme is illogical,' Baddi objected. 'Humans do not have the secret of advanced space travel. They do not possess the resources to reach even the nearest neighbouring star system. How can this new army of Malus be a threat?'

'I don't know – yet. But Zenia is not a fool,' said Adi. 'She must have a strategy. I would like to know what that strategy is. Wouldn't you?'

Baddi met Adi's gaze, impassive. Then she nodded. 'First, we must locate Zenia.'

'You already have,' said Adi coldly. 'Drone adapted the instruments on this station to scan for Malus DNA, and he's just found it. Zenia is based somewhere in Manhattan Island, New York City, in America.'

Drone didn't look pleased, or should I say, looked even less pleased than usual. 'How can you know this?'

'The instruments on this station receive signals from sensors mounted on the exterior.' Adi smiled thinly. 'I tapped the feeds and intercepted the information before it reached you. Once a scout, always a scout.'

'You're a badass,' I told Adi with a grin.

Adi blinked. 'My form is shaped incorrectly?'

'There's no such thing,' Jamila assured her.

'Look, finding Zenia is one thing,' I said. 'But if antimatter causes a massive explosion, how can you use it as a weapon without taking out New York?'

Ominously, Adi didn't answer.

Before I could take it further, we were interrupted by a piercing intermittent alarm and red warning lights erupting from the ISS monitors. Drone waved his hands over a keyboard and commands typed in by themselves. 'Major power surge,' he reported. 'There's a message incoming.'

Jamila hugged herself. 'From the Swarm?'

'From Zenia,' Drone said.

I felt a familiar chill just at the name. We all watched as the image of Zenia resolved on the screen. Or rather, something that may once have *looked* like Zenia. Me and Jamila flinched from the image: her features had grown longer, distorted; her neck looked thicker, wide as a horse's; the Blueteeth braces looked ready to ping free, concertinaed over yellowing fangs.

'Agents of the Swarm, hear us,' Zenia said, her voice low and gruff. 'Our sensors detected your scan. We know you have located us.'

'Then surrender,' Drone said. 'Abandon your plans.'

Zenia's smile was a crafty leer. 'You do not know our plans.'

'Irrelevant,' said Baddi. 'Your people are a part of the Swarm. Swarm technology must not be held by lesser races.'

'You will remove yourselves and your technology from this world,' Drone instructed. 'If you do not, your Swarm nation – all that survives of your civilisation – will face the harshest penalties.'

'You've heard of good cop, bad cop?' I whispered to Jam. 'Meet bad cop, even worse cop.'

'The Earth is neutral territory for us both,' said Zenia. 'We propose a summit here. Let us explain our grievances. Discuss terms face to face. If you do this, we will abide by the justice of the Swarm.'

'Very well,' said Drone. 'We shall come to you. At the first hint of treachery, you will be destroyed. You must know we have the means?'

'Oh, yes. We have detected your antimatter weapon,' said Zenia. 'Now we will send you coordinates of the rendezvous. We shall expect you.'

With a fizz of static, the image blinked off. There was a beep from the monitor and more numbers spilled across the screen.

Adi glanced at it and translated. 'The meeting place is

in Grand Central Station in midtown Manhattan.'

Jamila frowned. 'That's got to be, like, the most mega busy place for an alien meet in the world.'

'Zenia's base is located underneath it,' Drone said.

'Accessing online information,' Baddi announced. 'There are basements that extend for four-hundred-and-eighty thousand square metres below Grand Central Station, among the largest in New York City. Much of the space is said to be derelict. But they house an electrical substation which provides power for the station and its live rails.'

'Space for Malus to infest,' said Adi. 'Power that Zenia can draw on.'

'A ready-made secret underground alien lair,' I said miserably. 'Perfect.'

'And Zenia's expecting you,' Jamila said, turning to Agent Drone. 'You don't seriously think she wants to talk with you, do you? Last time she offered to chew the fat, Zenia ended up blowing you to bits.'

'At the first sign of treachery we will destroy her absolutely.' Drone prised the antimatter container from

Adi's arms. 'With this.'

'That thing!' I winced, half expecting it to go off. 'You'll kill millions of people!'

'Better than eight billion,' Baddi said with a pointed look in my direction. 'Perhaps the Swarm will be merciful to your kind, if we *can* remove all alien technology as we were ordered.'

'So what's the plan,' I demanded. 'Can you flux this antimatter stuff down to the planet surface?'

'It is too volatile,' Drone admitted. 'The smallest fluctuation in the electromagnetic field that shields it will cause it to destruct.'

'As will the stresses of our physically entering the atmosphere as before,' Baddi added.

'Such are the weaknesses of the physical form.' Drone grimaced. 'We will have to travel so slowly through the atmosphere that we do not create friction.'

'That's probably just what Zenia's depending on,' said Adi. 'I have another idea.'

'A safer idea?' I ventured.

Adi smiled. 'Hell, no.'

CHAPTER TWENTY-THREE
TARGET TO DESTROY

The International Space Station is a long-term base for crewed operations in space. It's not a vehicle. With high-tech stuff sticking out in all directions, it's the least aerodynamic thing you could imagine. It circles the Earth but it could never fly.

Of course it couldn't.

Which is why, right now, Adi and the two Swarm agents were steering it through the skies over the choppy Atlantic like their own private jet. Buffeted by turbulence, me and Jamila clung together, groaning and praying and holding the antimatter containment device between us. It looked like an oversized barbell made from brushed aluminium, the same space grey as an iPhone. And now we were back in the world of gravity it felt as heavy as a barbell three times its size. It felt weird being rooted to the floor again, but I was distracted by the way the central shaft of the barbell tingled to the touch. Or maybe that was just the vibration going through me as turbulence batted us about like a ball of wool attacked by an infinite number of cats.

'I'm still dreaming,' Jamila said, wide-eyed and shell-shocked as the steel and glass of the high-rise Manhattan skyline slowly came into view through the observation window. 'I ate something really gross at the back of the fridge and this is all a dream and I'm gonna wake up . . .'

'Or throw up,' I suggested, as the ISS dipped and lurched. Maybe gravity wasn't such a good thing.

We'd seen the blackness of space bleed into the blues and pinks of a new dawn on Earth – a view almost engulfed by impressive flames past the space station's cupola window as the whole structure did its best not to burn up in an atmosphere it was never designed to re-enter. With every jump and flip in our chaotic flight I kept checking the barbell, as if reassuring myself it was still there, it hadn't exploded, or imploded, or annihilated all matter for miles around without me noticing. That was our job:

to keep the containment device stable as far as possible. Meanwhile Baddi and Adi worked together to propel the ISS through the air by mental power alone, and Drone maintained a molecular shield around the station. This was meant to minimise the effects of re-entry from space, protect against atmospheric drag, keep our presence off the radar and basically to hold the station together as much as possible.

Clearly to do all that is a tough ask and even a digital alien superintelligence has limits. Drone said nothing, of course, but sweat poured from his face that had turned almost puce with the effort involved. Most of the solar panels had already broken away, and without them the instruments were flashing alarms, beeping and buzzing in a chorus of doom. We were rocking more and more, dipping more and more dramatically. I could only imagine what we must look like to the passengers on any passing planes: *Say, ain't that the International Space Station flying by? Must be astronauts on vacation . . .*

'How long do the batteries last without those panels?' Jamila asked me.

'Totally no idea,' I said. 'But hey, at least if life support goes we can stick our heads through the window.'

'I might have to do that anyway,' Jamila said, clutching her stomach with one hand. 'I think I'm gonna hurl.'

'You are not!' I told her. 'If you do, I'll—'

I never finished my threat, so not even I know what I'd have done. Because Agent Drone pointed and a massive explosion went off right beside us. The inside of the cabin flashed a brilliant, bloody red and shook like a sheet in the wind.

We dropped from the sky like a stone.

Adi raised one hand into the air and mimed a series of manoeuvres and our fall became a sharp, hard swerve to the left.

'What was that blast?' I screamed at Drone. 'What did you do?'

'He destroyed an AIM-9 heat-seeking air-to-air missile before it could destroy us,' Adi told me calmly. 'The missile was fired roughly thirty seconds ago from a F-22 Raptor stealth fighter jet scrambled from Langley Air

Force Base, Virginia.'

'Huh?' yelled Jamila. 'How can you know all that?'

'I have been monitoring signal traffic,' Adi said. 'As an unidentified flying object that has entered United States airspace without clearance, we have been designated maximum threat.'

'Unidentified?' I craned my neck to see out of the window. 'We're the International Space Station! Tell them, Adi!'

'The fighter jet's pilot has been insisting we identify ourselves and change course,' said Baddi calmly. 'Since changing our course would render our entire flight meaningless, there seemed little point in engaging—'

Drone jabbed out his arm again, at the other side of the ISS. There was another blast and shockwave from outside, and again everything shook – my legs especially.

'Looks like they're engaging *us* all right!' Jamila shouted.

The space station pitched violently towards the water, still travelling way too fast for comfort. It felt like we were a stone sent skipping over New York Harbour.

I found myself looking down on the Statue of Liberty's blue copper crown, with the stern front of the iconic skyline ahead of us.

'Tell the jet fighters you're carrying two helpless British teenagers,' Jamila said. 'And that we're carrying some heavyweight antimatter!'

'A second Raptor has been launched on an intercept course,' Drone announced through gritted teeth. 'Travelling at Mach 2.'

'That's twice the speed of sound,' Adi added helpfully.

'Speed increasing ,' said Baddi .

'They won't shoot us down,' I said. 'I mean, they'll see we have no weapons.'

'Duh, Danny-boy, we're a big lump of space debris flying supersonic towards Manhattan,' Jamila pointed out. 'We *are* the weapon!'

My heartbeat hit Mach 3 as a sleek fighter plane, broad and flat with two sharply rising tail fins, came thundering alongside us.

'Whoever's flying that doesn't need heat-seeking missiles now,' I said. 'They'll shoot us like fish in a barrel

– and if the antimatter goes boom . . .'

'Goodbye New York,' said Jamila.

'Adi,' I shouted, and they both nodded. 'Can you work the Raptor pilot's ejector seat from here?'

The next moment, the glass-and-metal canopy over the pilot jettisoned and a seat tore away upward into the sky, its parachute deploying almost immediately.

'Ejector seat engaged,' Adi confirmed. 'The Raptor itself will splashdown safely out to sea.'

'There goes a zillion US military dollars,' Jamila muttered.

I tried to see out the window, but we had already left the moment behind, screaming into the city. The East River ran like a dark artery through the body of Manhattan below. A thousand skyscrapers pointed up at us like accusing fingers.

Jamila looked guilt stricken. 'Will the pilot be OK?'

'The ACES II seat is optimised to limit human injuries at higher ejection dynamic pressure,' said Baddi, her voice glitching weirdly. 'But. We cannot sustain this structure's flight much longer.'

Me and Jamila chorused together: '*What?*'

'Third fighter jet approaching,' said Adi tersely.

'Energene levels . . .' Agent Drone was sweating so hard I thought his whole face might slide off on to his chest. 'Levels . . . dangerously depleted.'

'Can't sustain . . . ISS . . . structural integrity . . . much longer.' Baddi turned to look at us. She looked clammy and sick. 'Losing altitude.'

'The antimatter,' I said. 'If it detonates, we're all dead.'

'While Zenia survives,' said Jamila, 'deep down underground.'

'Mission failure . . . unacceptable.' Drone was shaking and the sweat was thrown from him like a dog shaking its coat. The ISS banked left, away from the river and through the steel-glass canyons of the city. A solar panel caught against the side of a building and both came off badly, debris showering over a building site adjacent. *At least whoever's down there's wearing hard hats*, I thought grimly. I glimpsed the Empire State Building up ahead. The ISS was the most incredible and expensive object ever built in Earth's history, and we were using it like a runaway sightseeing bus. Our altitude dipped down dangerously. Time seemed to slow. I could hear the blare of traffic in the streets below. Saw an aircraft clawing its way through the skies towards us.

And then I was barrelling over and over like I'd been thrown out of the window. I caught crazy corkscrews of sky, glass and red paving and then I struck something soft.

Something soft that said '*OWWWNODON'T YOU'LLSETITOFF!*'

'Jamila?' Dazed, I pushed myself up on my hands. 'Where . . . ?'

It was a fair question. Because we weren't inside the ISS any more. We were outside, on a warm, bright day. Jamila was curled up beside me, trembling, the barbell of antimatter clutched tight to her body like the world's worst comfort blanket, and we were perched on a smart and lengthy terrace near the top of a tall, tall building. All New York City was laid out before us through a glass barrier. We had pitched up together on an observation deck on top of a skyscraper, the kind where they charge tourists a fortune to enjoy the 360-degree view. The glass-fronted rooftop building across from us was branded, *Top of the Rock*. I'd heard of this place. Dad went one time – he mailed me pictures.

'This is the Rockefeller Centre,' I said, clocking the Empire State Building. 'Must be a stone's throw from where the ISS passed.'

'Adi's version of an ejector seat,' Jam whispered. 'She got us away.'

'Or Drone did,' I said, 'to protect the antimatter. If we crashed and set it off it could blow up the city—'

'But no guarantee of getting Zenia if she's deep underground.' Jamila got up, staring out at the crowded procession of skyscrapers all around and the river beyond. 'Danny, what's happened to the Adis and Drone the Moan? Where are they?'

'You know them, they're indestructible,' I told her. 'They'll be all right.'

'They weren't just now though, were they? They were ready to drop,' Jamila reminded me. 'And if their bodies pack up, there's nowhere they can go to print a new one!'

'We don't know the ISS is toast,' I argued.

'But look around!' Jamila went through three hundred and sixty degrees as if to demonstrate. 'There's no one here, on a lovely day. The building must've been evacuated.'

I nodded, looked around myself, trying to think straight. It was weirdly deserted up here like Jamila said. No one was around.

No, wait, there *was* someone. A grey-haired man in a security guard's uniform, coming out from the rooftop building. He was walking kind of slowly, strangely. Although who was I to judge? As I got shakily to my feet it was all I could do to stay on them.

'Excuse me,' I called. 'Did . . . something big happen?'

'No, but something's *going* to happen,' said the guard with a horrible smile, as two more guards came out to join him. 'You're both gonna die.'

'You will die in the name of Malus,' said the second security guard.

'In the name of Malus,' agreed the third.

No. No, no, no . . . I felt my world tilt. *After all we've been through . . . we're too late.* I clutched Jamila's arm.

'Zenia's started transmitting the DNA hack.'

'It'll spread through New York and from there . . . to everywhere.' Jamila looked at me. 'Zenia's won!'

The guards stepped menacingly towards us.

CHAPTER TWENTY-FOUR
NIGHTMARE OF NEW YORK

As the three guards moved closer, two thoughts cut through my building panic. Firstly, that the edge of an observation deck seventy floors up was not the best place to stand when people were coming to kill you, and secondly, that the guards were not fast movers. They were doing that kind of staggering zombie walk you see on horror flicks.

'Must be a side effect of the hack,' I said. 'Bodies not working properly.'

'I can show them how to run,' said Jamila. 'Split up? You go left, I'll go right.'

I nodded. The guards were already growing more confident in their movements. 'Who takes the antimatter?'

'*We* take it,' said the old guy.

That's what they want, I realised. *The only thing*

that can still stop Zenia.

'Now!' yelled Jamila, and she bolted away. The guards turned, made towards her – and I ran to my left. The observation deck ran around all four sides of the glass building in its middle, and so did I. By the time I reached the sliding doors, Jamila was already in ahead of me, standing at the elevators. The barbell was tucked under one arm and with her free hand she was stabbing at the call button.

The security guards were speeding up. The old man lurched through the sliding doors, his lean face fixed in concentration. The other two followed obediently.

I felt sick with adrenalin. 'Come on!' I growled, to the lift, to Jamila, to any guardian angels who might be listening. Finally, with a ping, the lift doors slid slowly open.

Hands lunged through the widening gap to grab us.

'Whoa!' Jamila jumped backwards and cannoned into me as six tourists staggered out of the lift, arms outstretched like they were zombies hungry for brains.

They were murmuring in different languages, but I heard one guy using English: 'You will die . . . you will die . . .'

'Stairs!' I shouted.

'Where?' Jamila looked round. The security guards were almost in reach.

'How should I—? *There*!' I saw an emergency-exit sign pointing further into the building. Ducking under a tourist's arm I ran for it. Fingers closed on Jamila's hood but she yelled and yanked herself free.

I threw open the door, gazing at a flight of concrete steps leading down to the next landing. 'What if we run into people on the stairwell?'

'This building's, like, a million storeys high,' Jam pointed out. 'Who in their right mind would ever take the stairs?'

'*No one* here's in their right mind,' I reminded her. But I threw myself after her, taking the steps down two at a time, gripping the bannister for support. The scuffle of our feet created a concerto on the concrete. I couldn't hear our pursuers; surely we'd outrun them?

After who-knows-how-many storeys I stopped to catch my breath. 'One sec,' I panted to Jamila.

'No time!' She gave me a look. 'Don't you wish YOU had taken athletics more seriously, Danny-boy?'

'Yes,' I freely admitted, and nodded to the barbell. 'How come you're still so fast even carrying that thing under your arm?'

'I'm trying to outrun it,' she deadpanned. 'Now can we shift?'

We could, and we did. My legs were tight and shaky, breath coming in shallow scrapes against the back of my throat, ears pummelled by the echo of our noisy footfalls. Jamila, weighed down with the containment device, was starting to tire at last and I made a childish point of pushing myself harder just to get past her.

So as I reached the landing of the twentieth floor it was me who ran into the big guy in the Hawaiian shirt. He showed no surprise, just lunged at me. I darted aside, banged into the stair rail and bounced off it, skittering past him. He ignored me completely and made for Jamila. Even as she skidded to a stop, he was bearing down on her.

'Jam!' I shouted, holding out my hands. 'The antimatter!'

With a gasp of effort she tossed the barbell over the man's head towards me. It seemed to take a lifetime to reach me but my sweaty hands closed tight on the brushed metal and I clutched it to my chest, falling back against the wall.

The man turned at once, eyes fixing murderously on me.

I'd been right. 'This is what they're after!' I shouted.

But the guy had turned his back on Jamila. Big mistake. She rammed into him and he fell against the wall. Then she grabbed my hand and pulled me after her.

'Gotta think,' she panted. 'Why was this place deserted? Maybe they started evacuating this whole area when the ISS showed up on the radar.'

'Or maybe if it's crashed?' I said between gasps of air. 'No, there wouldn't have been time . . .'

'And there still isn't,' Jamila said, as we heard heavy footsteps on the stairwell tumbling after ours. 'Just keep moving.'

Yeah, I thought helplessly. No energenes, no local knowledge, no plan at all. Just the two of us, hunted down for a weapon we didn't even know how to use by ordinary people turned into homicidal maniacs by the will of Malus.

Before we got as far as the ground floor I saw another door marked MAINTENANCE – NO ADMITTANCE. I hesitated. 'The main entrance could be overflowing with people,' I said. 'Maybe there's a quieter way—?'

The door burst open and two men in hard hats piled out from inside. Jamila swiped the shin of the one nearest her, knocking his feet out from under him – and in desperation I brained the other with the antimatter barbell. Even as he fell on top of his mate, I winced at the clang and cringed. 'God, Jam, I'm so sorry!'

'That we're still here? Me too,' she joked darkly. Before the maintenance door could close, she stepped through and started into the dingy corridor beyond. 'Maybe it's not real antimatter in there? Maybe it's *uncle*matter!'

I followed her, shaking my head. 'That joke was horrible.'

'My humour is on a higher plane, that's all.'

'Unless it's gonna airlift us out of here, your higher

plane can join that fighter plane at the bottom of the Hudson . . .'

We kept up the quiet banter as best we could, each trying to distract the other, making our way through a rabbit warren of corridors. Finally, we came out into an underground car park – or parking structure, I guess I should say. The vans and lorries there stood empty, many with their doors open, as if the occupants had simply got out and left.

'Come on,' I said, making for the exit. There was a barrier up ahead and a glass-walled office beside it where the car park attendants should've been. But it was empty.

'This doesn't feel right,' Jamila said.

'Gee, do you think?' I hissed. But as we reached the barrier, I could hear slow, scuffling footsteps to my right. A ton of them.

A big, straggling crowd of maybe fifty people was edging into sight.

'Run!' I yelled – like it needed saying, I know. But I have never been so terrified in my life. Jamila was already taking the left turn ahead of me on to the wide sidewalk running along West 50th Street. We raced past some fancy clothes store, and the big glass display windows cracked and shattered as more zombies came shuffling out to join the mob.

Finally the street gave on to 5th Avenue and we paused, panting for breath. The traffic had stopped. Cars stood empty. It was eerie as anything, especially with the rising soundtrack of moaning, shouting zombies out for our blood. Despite everything, my eyes were taken by the huge cathedral ahead of us, so out of place among the skyscrapers.

'Feel like praying?' I asked Jamila.

'In a Christian church? Not without a really good reason.' She looked past me, north up 5th Avenue, her eyes widening. 'And here it comes now.'

I turned. Fifty metres away, a big car jumped as if kicked by an invisible boot and barrel-rolled into a store window.

Behind it stood a mountain of a man, a huge and threatening figure in a dark suit. Even from this distance I could see the train-track braces on his misshapen smile.

'Alpha,' I breathed.

'Figures,' said Jamila.

'Because we know Zenia's here?'

'Because just when you think things can't get worse, they always do. Come on!'

Alpha strode towards us through the middle of the avenue. At a gesture, the car in front of him skidded away, crashing into an SUV with enough force to carry both clear across the sidewalk.

Me and Jamila ran faster along 5th Avenue, but he quickened his pace to match ours. Behind him, the herd of zombies came stumbling on. Every look back over my shoulder was pure nightmare.

Sprinting past Saks Fifth Avenue we came to an intersection. The Puma store on the corner of East 49th Street spat glass from its high-tech frontage. A bus twitched and skidded out to block the junction of West 49th Street opposite. We had to keep running down 5th Avenue, still so spookily deserted. Every breath was scraping the back of my throat, and I felt sick with effort. But somehow I kept going, and so did Jam. We made it another block, and this time a pyramid of yellow taxis piled up across the junction of East 48th Street, while the route west was blocked by another ragtag jumble of pedestrians, shambling towards us, ready to join the rabble taking their lead from Alpha.

'They're herding us,' Jamila panted. I could see tears in her eyes even as she wiped them furiously. 'Making sure we go this way.'

I chanced an exhausted glance behind and found Alpha still sweeping abandoned vehicles out of his way. Powerful, commanding, a possessed army massed at his back. Jamila was right, he *was* herding us. I didn't like the thought of that.

Two fire hydrants on opposite sides of West 45th Street suddenly burst, firing giant jets of water at each other, meeting with a colossal storm of spray in the middle. Biting my lip I started towards it anyway – what's a little water, right? – but then two food trucks and a shelter for outdoor diners slithered like living things out into the road, blocking it entirely.

'No choice,' I grunted.

We half ran, half staggered down East 45th Street. It passed in a grey blur, quiet and deserted, until we reached Madison Avenue.

Then we saw what was waiting for us ahead.

You know I described the crowd of zombies on our tails? Well, here was a full-on stadium's worth. Hundreds and hundreds of people, rammed up close together, standing and staring at us in sinister silence. They didn't move. Didn't speak. It was like they were extras on the set of a disaster movie waiting for the cue to action.

Me and Jamila, we stopped running. Heaving for breath, we couldn't even speak. But then, we didn't have to. The hopeless looks we swapped said just about everything.

Behind us we heard the crash and crump of cars twisting aside so as not to obstruct Alpha's army. I turned, saw the big man march into sight.

The hordes ahead of us must have seen him too. And with that sighting, they broke into a stumbling run towards us. Sensing victory or scenting blood, Alpha's rabble quickened their step. Some fell, to be trampled by the others who overtook their leader, as if desperate to reach us first.

'Trapped,' I gasped, as if Jamila hadn't noticed.

'We tried,' she said simply.

And then she hugged me, and I hugged her back and shut my eyes, as the mob closed in to destroy us.

CHAPTER TWENTY-FIVE
POKING THE ANTS' NEST

Of course I couldn't stop hoping. Right to the end. I imagined Adi swooping out from the sky like Captain Marvel to whisk me and Jam away from danger. Or a hidden store of energenes bursting from Jamila at the last moment to protect us, or the barbell we'd been lugging all this way suddenly crackling into magical life and striking down Alpha's army.

Of all the things I imagined coming to my rescue, Agent Drone really wasn't one of them. And yet, as the mob of possessed humans converged around us, they were suddenly thrown backwards. The ground shook and then shattered, and cement dust and concrete burst upward like water from a whale's blowhole. Drone rose through the hole in the middle of the road, threw his arms around me and Jam and crushed us to his chest. Then he jumped with us both back down through the hole.

There was barely time to brace for impact. When it came it was sharp and savage. Agent Drone landed on his feet and I was jarred free, landing on wet tiles beside Jamila. *The barbell*, I thought desperately. *I've lost it!* But before the daylight above was shut off and a patch of thick tarry stone sealed the split, I saw the antimatter containment device clutched in Drone's huge hand.

He turned his back on us and walked away without another word. It was the barbell he'd come to rescue. Not us.

'Hey!' I shouted, unable even to sit. I was so tired, full of cramps, exhaustion sucking at my soul even as refrigerator temperatures underground goosefleshed my skin. But no way was I just gonna be ignored. 'What happened? Where's Adi?'

A hand appeared out of the darkness in front of me. Dark eyes sparkled into my own. 'I'm glad to see you, Danny. And you, Jamila.'

There she was. I looked up at her and nodded. 'Glad you made it.'

'Yeah,' Jamila panted. 'But d'you think some day you could rescue us *before* the nick of time?'

'This may be the last day your race will know,' said Adi softly. 'Come. We must leave here.'

I took her hand and let her pull me to my feet. 'Where are we? Subway? Sewer?'

'A minor tunnel running through Grand Central Station's underground basement complex.'

I stared. 'We're near Grand Central?'

'The terminal building is close above us,' said Adi. 'I tried to put you down as close to it as possible.'

'Average work,' said Jamila. 'Must try harder. See me.'

Adi helped her up too. 'You're funny, Jamila.'

'Thanks,' said Jamila. 'Where's Drone the Moan gone in such a hurry?'

'To locate the transmitter,' Adi said. 'If we find that, we find Zenia. That is his belief.'

'Taken you long enough, hasn't it?' I said, a bit indignantly. 'We were all alone out there.'

'I'm so sorry, Danny. The journey here exhausted our

energenes. We have been forced to recharge from the Grand Central electrical substation.' Adi helped Jamila up and then paused. 'Well, Baddi and Drone have done so. I mostly took energy from the ISS.'

'You drained the batteries?' I asked.

'I ate the astronaut meals,' Adi confessed. 'The Kung Pao chicken was particularly good.'

It felt a lifetime since I'd last eaten, but my stomach was too tight with tension to consider filling it. 'So, are you back to full strength?'

'Far from it,' Adi confessed. 'But my . . . associates do not anticipate a physical struggle now we have the antimatter unit.'

Over Adi's shoulder I was amazed to see dim lights glowing from inside what was left of the International Space Station, half impacted in the ground, one stubborn solar sail bent against the tunnel roof. 'Speaking of the antimatter unit,' I said, 'you dumped us with it cos you had to flux underground before you hit the street, and you worried that might set off the big boom, am I right?'

'Yes, Danny. The alternative was to crash the ISS

into the tarmac at ninety-seven miles per hour, and that might've tickled. Now, quickly.' Adi stalked away along the tunnel after Agent Drone, and with a shrug we had to follow.

'She's sassing you, Danny-boy,' said Jamila. 'I feel I've taught her well . . .'

Soon we passed the downed ISS. The last of its light died away and then Baddi stepped out from the wreck, all but licking her lips. She raised her hand and it glowed with light, illuminating the way ahead. The 'tunnel' had a vaulted roof with dirt-caked tiles, and from the markings on the stony ground I guessed that train tracks had been pulled up from here long ago, perhaps when a line was shut down or diverted. I wondered how it would link up with the rest of the terminal, and if even now a party of zombified humans were making their way through the darkness towards us.

'This is a rubbish tour of New York City,' I said. 'I want my money back.'

'I have observed how you attempt to lighten moments of fear and despair with humour,' Baddi said at length. 'This is a pointless activity. It cannot affect the outcome of events.'

'Aw, you take all the fun out of it,' I said drily.

'Now you're sassing her, like Adi sassed you. I can't keep up.' Jamila mock sighed. 'Joking apart, how come me and Danny aren't Malus zombies right now? I mean if Zenia's got her transmitter working . . .'

'For the same reason Zenia couldn't control my thoughts on the train when I came after you,' I reckoned. 'Adi put protections in our brain first time around.'

'If she did, they didn't help. My mind was still changed. My *body* was changed.'

'That change was forced into you through repeated digiscanning and bodyprinting,' Adi called back. 'Now all Malus DNA has been removed from you, your protection continues. Yours continues too, Danny.'

'Well, good,' said Jamila. 'I don't want to turn horrible again. I want to stay *me*.'

'No one wants Jamalien back. Your breath was horrible,' I joked. But I had to admit the thought of losing my will scared the hell out of me too, for all Adi's reassurances.

The tunnel branched off in three different directions. As if following a scent, Adi led us through the walkway to the left which trailed gently downward. Our footsteps crumped against the old, cold stone in muffled echoes.

'So do the zombies staying human mean that Zenia's totally fixed the mutation thingy?' asked Jamila. 'Humans will stay human at least, even if they're under her control?'

'The process will be unreliable,' Baddi said. 'The transmitter depends on Swarm components to function at full efficiency. Using human substitutes, Zenia has only been able to influence the population of this urban area. Approximately eight million people.'

'*Eight million?*' I stopped so short, Jamila walked into the back of me. 'That many?'

'The transmission area currently covers over two thousand square kilometres,' Adi confirmed. 'The population of most of New York City's five boroughs has been affected to greater or lesser extents, causing widespread panic and disruption.'

'Most are not yet under Zenia's active control,' said

Baddi. 'They are merely in a vegetative state while the transmitted code works to make them obey.'

'But here, nearer the transmitter, they're already taking orders,' said Jamila. 'The streets were so quiet cos she'd ordered most of her "army" to guard her base at Grand Central, right?'

'Zenia was driving us there,' I said. 'Or driving the antimatter there, anyway.'

'But then why did her Alpha slave not pursue you and try to take it?' Adi wondered aloud. 'There are thousands of humans under Malus control above us, ready to fight and die at Zenia's command.'

'I have told you, her strategy is illogical,' Baddi insisted. 'A likely product of mental instability, self-inflicted through her experiments.'

'And *your* problem is, you've got a brainache brought on by downloading too many dictionaries,' Jam grumbled. 'Don't underestimate Zenia. Or the Malusonians.' She rubbed the back of her head. 'I know they've gone from me now, but I can still remember the feelings underlying everything . . .' She shrugged, struggling to sum it up.

'Anticipation. Vengeance. And . . . *hunger*.'

I felt chills go through me and gave Jamila's arm a squeeze. 'Try not to think about it.'

'Because it's freaking you out?'

'Basically.' I walked a little faster to keep pace with Baddi. 'So what are we going to do?'

'We must use the antimatter to destroy all non-earth technology,' said Baddi. 'You did well to keep it from her.'

I actually blushed at the simple compliment.

Jamila mouthed a sarcastic 'OMG' and pretended to fan her face. 'Can you fire that barbell like a gun?' she asked. 'Can you use, like, just a bit of the antimatter, or is it gonna blow up everything – and us with it?'

'The annihilation will release huge amounts of energy, comparable to the heat flash and shockwave of a nuclear bomb,' said Baddi, 'vaporising everything and everyone within a radius of one-point-three kilometres.'

'No way,' I said. 'You can't.'

'We can,' Baddi assured me.

'But the death count, the casualties . . .'

'*Malusonian* casualties, now,' said Baddi. 'You wished

for us to get involved, Danny. We *are* involved.'

'And what about us?' Jamila challenged her. 'We're involved too. What happens to us when this thing goes off?'

'If you remain sheltered further underground you might survive,' said Baddi, sounding so matter of fact she could've been talking about a round of sandwiches. 'At least the annihilation will leave no radioactive fallout in the area.'

'But there has to be another way.' I pushed past Baddi to catch up with Adi. 'You can't let her do this.'

'We must do what needs to be done, Danny,' Adi told me quietly. 'When the time comes—'

Before Adi could finish her words, a shadow loomed ahead of us. It was the dark, massive figure of Drone. Light glowed from the fingertips of his left hand, and in his right hand he held the barbell. Ignoring me and Jamila – and Adi for that matter – he told Baddi, 'I have traced the signals from the code transmitter: its location is thirty-three metres above us.'

'Is it shielded?' Baddi asked.

POKING THE ANTS' NEST

'Unknown,' he answered. 'I must establish that it will be vulnerable to our antimatter attack . . . and that Zenia herself is also within the strike area.'

'The energenes she possesses may be enough to project her outside the instant kill zone,' Baddi agreed. 'We must be sure Zenia dies with her deranged plans.'

'I will locate her,' said Adi, stepping between them. 'I am the scout. The original.'

'The inferior,' said Baddi primly. 'And therefore, more expendable.'

'Give me the antimatter device,' Adi persisted. 'I will employ it as soon as I see her, allowing you to remain safely—'

'No, Scout. You cannot be trusted to work independently. You are unreliable. You lack unity with the Swarm.' Drone dismissed her and turned to Baddi. 'It will take fifty seconds to power down the electromagnetic field within the containment device and so bring matter and antimatter into collision. Before I can do so, you – and your earlier version – must locate Zenia. If she is within the kill zone, you will signal me and keep her there. We must ensure that nothing can interrupt the countdown . . .'

While they were making their plans, I huddled closer to Jamila. 'Listen to them. Even if we win, we lose – cos they're gonna murder millions of helpless people!'

Jamila nodded miserably. 'Still. How many more will be transformed into Zenia's soldiers if they don't?'

'I know.' I heaved out a sigh. 'Not like we can even do anything. They don't care what we think. We were just packhorses for their precious antimatter while it suited them . . .'

Then a low rumble built suddenly into what felt like a minor earthquake. It shook the passageway and brought a shower of rock dust down from the ceiling.

'What was that?' hissed Jamila.

The passage rocked again and this time I yelled as a huge chunk of the roof above us fell to the ground and broke by my feet. 'Cave-in!' I shouted.

Drone ignored me, staring at Adi and Baddi. 'You have your instructions. Go.'

'Adi!' Jamila yelled as the vibration rumbled around

us again. She pushed me aside as a huge metal spear thrust down from above as if to skewer us.

It was the tail end of a helicopter. What the hell was happening?

Then Adi's fingers slipped into mine and she closed her eyes. 'Let us go above ground.' I felt the familiar turn of my guts, the tug at my soul.

And then we fluxed, and the crumbling tunnel was left behind. I felt sun on my skin. Smoke blew across my face and I stared round, terrified. We were on a crowded pedestrian plaza. Hundreds of people stumbled around the twisted remains of a fire engine and a police helicopter, but none of them seemed to have noticed us. Yet.

Baddi appeared beside us. 'You should have left the children behind,' she told Adi quietly. 'They have no special abilities and we are too weak to share our powers with them. They are useless.'

'Thanks,' I said with a look at Jamila.

'Danny and Jamila are never useless,' Adi informed Baddi. 'They are under my protection.'

'And those tunnels we were in must be right under

here,' said Jamila, pointing to the wrecked copter.

With a chill, I saw that its tail was missing. 'I guess Alpha's still after us,' I said quietly. 'Stabbing us with bits of emergency vehicles. Nice touch.'

Another helicopter appeared, circling overhead. As one, a large crowd began to scatter, stumbling away to clear an area the size of a tennis court. The helicopter stopped circling, hanging in the sky like metal fruit from the clouds. Then, as if plucked by giant invisible fingers, it rocketed straight down into the patch of plaza the zombies had vacated. The crash was horrific – the impact almost knocked me to my knees. And even as the copter exploded, it fluxed out of sight, the echoes of the blast fading to nothing.

'Guess we know where that thing's gone,' said Jamila, staring at the scorched concrete.

'Zenia must still think we're underground,' I said.

Baddi looked back at me. 'No.'

I realised that the possessed people crowding the plaza had stopped milling about. They were staring at the four of us.

'Welcome,' came a rasping voice.

It was Zenia.

At the sight of her, my heart threw grappling hooks up my throat, ready to haul itself out. She had emerged from one of Grand Central's covered entrances, standing beneath a jolly red-and-white striped awning. But her mutation had grown worse. Her body had grown larger but her back was hunched over and her powerful limbs were warped and twitching. Her skin had turned tight and shiny with a green tint to it, and tufts of red hair sprouted in patches from a scabby scalp.

'Like poking sticks into an ants' nest, we have brought out the insects,' Zenia said, her Blueteeth implants glowing as she smiled. 'Ready to be stamped on.'

CHAPTER TWENTY-SIX
TRANSFORMATION

Insects, I thought. That was kind of rich coming from her! I kept picturing the Malusonian corpse in the chained-up bodyprinter, the remains of Zenia version two-point-one – the most terrifying thing I'd ever seen, even dead. What would a living Malusonian be like?

'All we need now is the other Swarm agent,' Zenia continued, 'and we can end this.'

'Yes,' shouted Baddi. 'We can.' She brought up her hands and tugged two granite blocks from out of Grand Central's wall like they were giant teeth for extraction. But Baddi was still weakened, and while she tried to bring them crashing down on Zenia she was too slow. Instead, Zenia held the stones in mid-air and then hurled them back at me and Jamila. Adi and Baddi swept their arms in the same direction and the huge blocks crashed through the marbled reception of an enormous skyscraper behind us.

The crowds on the plaza were suddenly animated with purpose. They were snarling like animals, closing in. And yet they weren't attacking. Not yet, anyway. Just shuffling closer.

'They're trying to intimidate us,' Adi said.

'Why not come inside out of their way?' called Zenia, her dark eyes glistening. She backed away into the Terminal building, beckoning to us.

'She's confident,' I observed with a bad feeling.

Adi looked at Baddi. 'She's within range of the antimatter blast. Have you signalled to Drone that it's time?'

'The agent will be here.' Baddi nodded. 'Come on. The containment device must be powered down before the antimatter can be unleashed. We will need to keep Zenia occupied.'

'Until we're all annihilated? Great,' I said bitterly. 'Maybe we should just start running now.'

But Adi took my hand and her fingers started tapping Morse code on the back of it.

- .-. ..- ... -

Jamila noticed the covert dance of Adi's fingers and whispered in my ear: 'What did she say?'

'*TRUST*,' I whispered back. But as the crowding zombies stumbled nearer, I knew it wasn't going to be easy.

'Inside,' said Baddi, focussed on the station entrance as if she could see through the pale stone; she probably could. 'Now.'

'Gladly,' I muttered.

With Jamila beside me, I followed Adi and Baddi inside this huge, stately station. My flesh crawled at the thought of the whole city full of people changing a little more with every passing minute, becoming unquestioning slaves to an alien will. It was horrible – but I knew that whatever was waiting for us inside was likely worse. And Agent Drone would surely start counting down to antimatter annihilation any moment now. What was Adi planning to do?

Could I trust her any more?

I kept looking back over my shoulder but at least the mob didn't follow us inside the building. Their growls and snarls grew fainter.

Grand Central Station was caked in crystal chandeliers and creamy yellow limestone, with a floor of perfectly polished marble. After crossing a deserted food court we entered the main concourse, which stood vast and eerily deserted. Its sheer size, with archways leading off in all directions towards different platforms and subway lines, would have made even the saddest soul want to soar – on any normal day.

But the silence was oppressive; it felt all wrong in a place built for bustle. The escalators were still. Sunlight fell in white streamers through huge arched windows. An American flag as big as a squash court hung above us. Twin marble stairways stretched up to an impressive upper level, more opera house than railway station. High, high above was a blue barrelled ceiling, with constellations of the zodiac picked out in gold leaf.

I looked up at the stars and thought, *It's your fault we're here.*

Jamila nodded towards the many-sided information booth with its huge ornamental clock. 'Maybe we should ask someone where Zenia is?'

'We are here.' Zenia stepped into sight on an upper gallery above the stopped escalators straight opposite us. A huge spherical chandelier hung over her, casting surgical brightness on her warped body. In a hall behind her, I could see a tall shard of metal mounted in a lattice of steel and cables and glowing like Zenia's Blueteeth braces.

'The transmitter,' I breathed.

Adi lashed out with her hand and the transmitter crumpled in on itself. I felt a wave of joy and relief as the light bled out from it. I almost punched the air.

But Zenia didn't react. She went on staring at us.

Baddi made a cutting motion with her hand and the chandelier above Zenia broke on its long cable and started to fall.

Almost lazily, Zenia raised a hand and the chandelier stopped falling. She held it for a few seconds until, with a contemptuous gesture, she tossed it over the balcony. The chandelier exploded, shards skittering across the smooth marble towards us.

'Broken into a billion pieces,' Zenia called, the airy echoes adding layers to her voice. 'Much like your hopes of stopping me—'

Her gloating stopped as marble tumbled away from beneath the balcony she stood on and in a cloud of dust she fell through it. The sunlight made the air opaque; when the air cleared I hoped to see Zenia's body sprawled across the escalator, an easy catch for Adi and Baddi.

But no. She was hovering in the air. Serene and unassailable.

'You creatures of the Swarm. You think your unity is so powerful. So important.' Zenia's face twisted into an ugly sneer. 'But sheep stay in groups. Lions prowl alone!'

Raising her arms, she sailed across the sunlit space towards us.

Jamila clutched my arm in terror. 'Someone take her down!'

'Can't,' hissed Adi, though she looked to be trying. 'Zenia is shielding herself from direct attack.'

'Then why didn't she shield her transmitter?' I said.

Baddi pointed to one of the great windows. It splintered into lethal shards and Adi propelled them through the air like a thousand glittering daggers. But Zenia slowed their movement so she soared past them before they could strike.

With a twist of her hand, the station's grand brass clock was squeezed off its perch like a grape from its vine. Powered through the air, one of its four faces smashed into Baddi's skull. She fell beside me with a thump, out cold it seemed, and I yelled in alarm. Because Zenia wasn't done with the clock: she was casting it round like a big brass bowling ball.

Again it thumped down on Baddi's body with colossal force. I saw dark liquid stain her silver hair. As I stepped forward, terrified, the clock knocked my legs from under me. Jamila tumbled down too. Zenia was playing with us. Laughing at us.

Adi launched herself into the air and flew at Zenia, crashing into her with enough force to knock her backwards. The pair grappled and began trading blows. Adi struck Zenia with both fists, hammering her to the ground. Zenia bounced straight up again and her hands closed around Adi's throat.

'Come on, Jam,' I hissed. 'We've got to do something to help.'

'Like what?' Jamila looked as terrified as I felt. 'She's right, we are ants to her. And to the Swarm. Everyone!'

'Ants can bite,' I reminded her. 'Even if we just distract her for a moment it might buy Adi time to land a blow that counts. Come on, while they're busy.'

Adi was thrown against the information booth and smashed through its roof. Zenia swooped down on her. I grabbed Jamila by the arm and pulled her along after me.

'Where are we headed?' she said.

'The balcony she was standing on,' I said. 'Why did she wait for us there?'

Jamila thought as we took the steps up two at a time. 'You think she was planning to use something?'

'Let's check it out,' I said.

Adi and Zenia were still locked in battle, spiralling up from the ruins of the information booth to fight it out among the golden stars in the ceiling high above.

Adi swung Zenia head-first into the brickwork, bringing down a shower of painted sky and stars. Zenia dropped like one of the stones and fell with an echoing crash. The impact sent a crack zigzagging through the marble floor away from her sprawled body. But then she hissed and rolled over, bloodied but ready again to fight. Adi blurred and vanished, reappeared down on the ground, keeping her distance maybe fifty metres from Zenia. She clutched her head dizzily.

'Danny!' Jamila hissed. 'Look!'

She wasn't staring at Adi and Zenia like I was. She was pointing to the far end of the ruined balcony we stood on. Two struggling figures barged into sight, both wearing dark suits.

'Alpha,' I breathed. 'And Agent Drone!'

Both 'men' looked bruised and battered. Alpha's skin was sallow and wet with sweat, cold fury burning in his eyes. Drone still held the antimatter barbell in one bloody hand and brought his free fist down on Alpha's skull. Alpha fell to his knees, lunged for Drone's left leg and twisted hard. Drone fell backwards and Alpha climbed on to him, trying to pin him to the marble.

'Here!' I yelled. 'Drone – uh, Mr Agent, I mean – the barbell, quick. Don't let Alpha get it.'

Drone craned his head, looking back at me. His face was scored with cuts and bruises but he showed no pain. He simply nodded.

Pushing one foot into Alpha's stomach he pushed his attacker away – and lobbed the barbell to me. I backed away, the better to catch it, but caught my heel on a lump of broken brick.

I could feel myself lose my balance. Time seemed to slow. As I fell backwards the barbell sailed out of my reach.

Thank God for Jamila, who reached up and caught it with both hands, holding it to her chest.

'We've got it!' I cheered.

But Drone was in no state to appreciate the news. Alpha's form was shifting, changing. The man who had once been Petr Loborik, his old life long-lost, was becoming something truly alien. With a sound like wet sticks snapping, his already muscular form elongated. His skull swelled up like a balloon; his eyes bulged, becoming black and beady.

'Alpha's going full Malus,' hissed Jamila.

Drone seemed unfazed. He lunged forward and pinned his opponent to the ground as Alpha's lengthening insectoid body writhed and twitched. Two pairs of thick insect arms closed around Drone's ribs and started to squeeze. The Swarm agent gasped.

'Danny, look out!' Adi shouted from the concourse. I dragged my gaze back to her battle in time to realise that it was over – Adi was on her knees beside Baddi's prone body, and Zenia was powering towards me. Desperately I threw myself aside but at the last moment Zenia changed course and targeted Jamila instead.

She snatched at the antimatter containment device.

Jam put up a fight. She held on to the barbell fiercely, even when Zenia lifted her into the air. But it was only ever going to end one way: Jamila lost her grip and dropped to the marble eight metres below. I threw myself towards her to help break her fall. We wound up sprawled on the walkway, clinging together.

I stared in horror at Zenia as she landed behind Alpha

and Drone as they struggled, the barbell held above her head. I hadn't wanted the Swarm to use the antimatter, but now that Zenia had it . . .

'This is it,' I hissed to Jamila.

'Game over,' she agreed.

Only it wasn't.

Calmly, Zenia turned and placed the barbell down on the floor. Then, with a casual gesture, she sent it skittering away over the marble.

'Surprised, Danny?' Zenia rasped. 'You think we wanted that silly little toy?' She shook her head. 'No. The antimatter . . . *doesn't* matter.'

I swapped a baffled look with Jamila. 'Then, what does?'

'This,' said Zenia, pointing to Agent Drone still in the grip of the Malusonian Alpha.

Drone's struggles were weakening; he was like a fly in a web straining to be free. 'This is what matters: an agent of the Swarm, weakened close to death.' She reached into her jacket pocket and pulled out something like a weird steel headband. Then she placed it around

Alpha's head and it glowed spookily. Soon, a green shimmering lightshow flickered and played around both him and Drone.

'Danny, Jamila, get away.' Adi was back on her feet. 'This is why Zenia took the scans of Swarm DNA at the house. She needed them to make *this* happen!'

'Make what happen?' I yelled.

'Don't leave now, children,' Zenia rasped. 'Stay and watch as the plans of Malus conclude at last.'

I stared in horror as the unearthly glow around the two figures grew more intense. It was hard to see where Swarm agent ended and Malusonian began.

'They're . . . *joining together*,' Jam whispered.

'You see it now, don't you, Scout – why it makes no difference that you shut down the transmitter. It had already played its part in our plans.' Zenia laughed. This is what we wanted. What we needed.' She gave a deep, guttural guffaw. 'What we knew would come to us in the end.'

'Adi,' I yelled across the empty concourse. 'What does she mean?'

In a heartbeat, Adi had fluxed to our side. 'The transmitter . . . Zenia never cared that it's only short-range. Possessing humanity was just a lure. A trap to bring us here!'

'We know your fondness for the humans, Scout. We knew you could not – *would* not – allow the Swarm to destroy them from outer space. So we staged our little coup here to give you the hope you could stop us and save this backwards planet once again.'

Jamila was frowning hard. 'Then, you never really wanted an army of humans?'

'Of course not. Restricted to this world as your people are, they are of no use to us,' Zenia agreed, looking again at Adi. 'We only threatened them to give the scout something to fight for. A means to persuade your fellows to deal with us here, in person.' Zenia's laugh was a slobbering cackle. 'We knew you would come, weak and exhausted in your flesh-being. That you would make it so much easier for us.'

'Stop talking in riddles,' I snapped. 'What have you done? What's that headset thing you put on Alpha?'

'It emphasises the will of Malus,' said Adi. Her eyes were dark and empty. 'The DNA hack attack on humanity was only a practice run. Don't you see?'

I shook my head dumbly.

'Me, Baddi, Drone,' said Adi. 'We are Swarm code dressed up in human bodies.'

Jamila swore under her breath. 'The Malusonians can hack human bodies . . .'

'And through that, take control of the digital DNA of the Swarm!' Adi said. 'The scans at the house made it clear to her – Swarm cells are pure and rigid, impervious to M-DNA. But when we take flesh-being, *human* DNA makes us more vulnerable. It acts as the glue between our incompatible cells . . .'

The glow was fading from Alpha and Agent Drone. I stared, sickened and repulsed. Two bodies had become one: a grotesque parody of Drone's form, twisted and distorted as if made from wet clay, with bulging compound eyes. Part Malusonian, part-Swarm agent. And all under Zenia's control.

She was almost shaking with rapture. 'With agents of

the Swarm under our control we will gain access to every secret of the Hive Mind. We will find a way to liberate the Malus Swarm nation and take control.' Zenia's voice rose to an exultant shriek. *'Each and every swarm will be ours!'*

CHAPTER TWENTY-SEVEN
SWARMUS RISING

'Let her gloat,' Adi whispered urgently. 'Baddi and I must have time to regenerate.'

'What's the use,' I muttered. 'You can't fight her. She's got what she wanted.'

'Not all of it,' said Adi. 'Not yet.'

It seemed Jamila was still trying to reason it out. 'Alpha equals human plus Malusonian. Agent Drone equals human plus Swarm. And so human DNA bridges the gap between the Swarm and Malus.'

'Right,' I agreed. 'And now they're bonded together. Mentally and physically.'

'And horribly,' Jamila added. 'It's a *Swarmus*.'

It was a name as nasty as the creature looked. The Swarmus got up unsteadily. It stood nearly three metres tall, clear gloop glistening on its skin, chest rising and falling as it whooped down air like a newborn thing. I couldn't stop staring at it, transfixed in horror.

Perhaps Zenia recognised the disgust on my face. 'The physical form is of no importance,' she said coldly.

'Well, you tried hard enough to get the antimatter from us,' I reminded her, 'cos you knew your physical form would be blown to bits.'

'A safeguard,' said Zenia. 'It would not be logical for the Swarm to trigger the device until they were sure we were within range.' She sniggered, a sound like a crocodile chewing meat. 'That relentless logic – and total predictability – will lead to the downfall of their empire.'

The Swarmus turned to Zenia and bowed his head. It wasn't just a nod of subservience; he was offering her the metal headset, the thing that had helped Alpha mesh fully with Drone.

'We know you have been seeking to delay us, Scout.' Zenia carefully removed the sticky headset. 'We suppose you hope to regenerate your energenes fast enough to defeat us. That hope is misjudged. But we have indulged you only while we waited for Alpha's bonding to be permanent.' She placed the steel band around her forehead. 'Now we can begin the second and final bonding.'

I looked at Jamila, then across the concourse to where Baddi lay, prone and helpless.

'No.' Adi still looked weak but there was such determination in her face. 'You will not take me – you will not take *her*.'

'We cannot take you. Your link to the Swarm has been severed.' Zenia's face was sweating, skin growing translucent as if something bubbled beneath. She looked across at Baddi. '*This* scout is loyal, unimaginative, obedient. It – *she* – will offer little resistance. With the access of an agent and the reach of a scout, there are few parts of the Hive we will not breach.'

Adi shook her head. 'The firewall Guardians will not let you pass.'

'You know the back ways into the Swarm,' Zenia gloated. 'Now *we* shall know them too—' Abruptly her body twisted and she screamed. I stared, mute, unable to tear my eyes away as the bones in her legs stretched and pushed out against her skin. She turned her back on us, and through her jacket I saw her spine rippling with new bulk.

'She's going full Malus too,' I said to Jamila, 'just in time for bonding.'

But Adi had something to say about that, and her hands said it for her. She sent fierce light scorching from her palms, and for a second Zenia staggered back.

Then the Swarmus leapt at Adi with horrible speed. His momentum knocked her off her feet and they crashed together through the stone wall of the balcony and down on to the floor. Like a golem, unhurt and undestroyable, he got up and loomed over her.

'Adi!' I yelled.

The Swarmus picked her up with one misshapen hand and hurled her across the concourse into a destination board. It exploded into sparks and shards of plastic. I saw Adi try to hover out of reach, but the Swarmus performed another bionic leap and plucked her out of the air. Adi was slam-dunked on the marble with a thump loud enough to shake the remaining glass in the high arched windows. Then the Swarmus kicked her body out of sight into a passageway.

I felt so useless. No energenes, no way to make a difference. Desperate, I picked up bits of broken brick and hurled them at the monster. Perhaps I could distract him – make him come after me, give Adi some breathing space. I tried to channel my anger, use it to give me strength. But it was no use: the stones fell short, the Swarmus was too far away. 'Jamila,' I said desperately, 'you're better at throwing than me, see if you can—'

'Danny, no. Look.' Jamila pulled me down into a crouch on the walkway, and my eyes were wrenched back to the horror of Zenia's transformation. It was as if the dried-out Malusonian corpse had come back to life and hopped continents to Grand Central, quivering with power. Zenia's prominent forelimbs bent and flexed.

'Hold still,' Jamila hissed.

The insectoid head tilted to one side as it surveyed us. But if it saw us at all, it found us of no interest. Its large black eyes fixed on Baddi.

'Move, Baddi!' I screamed at her.

Jamila yelled too: 'Move! *Move!*'

Zenia was already launching through the air. She took the eight-metre fall in her stride, landing lightly on fresh-formed limbs. Then she scuttled closer to her prey.

'Don't just lie there!' Jamila bawled.

Maybe Baddi finally heard. As Zenia lunged towards her, Baddi sat bolt upright and clapped her hands together with incredible force. Zenia was blown upward by the unexpected shockwave, shattering chandeliers before slamming into the roof. Plaster rained down and tremors shook through the whole building, and me and Jamila had to hold on to each other as our damaged walkway shook ominously.

Baddi fell back where she lay. She must have put everything she had into one final counterattack.

It wasn't enough. Zenia's Malusonian form clung to the ruins of a chandelier, staring down at her prey. She all but licked her chops.

One of the supporting columns beneath our balcony cracked and sagged. The floor lurched again, causing the antimatter containment device to topple on to its side. It started to roll, heading for the missing part of the balcony, ready to drop down to the concourse below. If the shock of the impact disrupted that magnetic field . . .

I ran and threw myself forward to block the barbell's path, palms stinging on the fractured marble. The containment device rolled to a stop against my body. 'I got it, Jam!' I gasped.

'Yeah, you got it.' Jamila looked at me, dark eyes wide. 'You've got a weapon. The only thing we have left.'

She pointed back to the concourse. Swarmus had re-emerged, dragging Adi behind him by her leg, which was clearly broken. Adi wasn't moving, her eyes were closed. Zenia had dropped silently back to the floor and now she chittered to Swarmus in her own language. He dropped Adi and lumbered closer to Baddi. I prayed she was shamming again, willed her to wake and fight back, to make these obscene creatures pay. But this time Baddi was down for real. To be sure, Swarmus stamped his huge foot down on her ribs. She didn't stir.

Zenia crept closer.

'Stop!' I bellowed.

Swarmus looked up at me. Zenia looked up at me. With a trembling arm I held the barbell over my head.

'Just back off,' Jamila yelled. 'Or he fires that thing.'

Zenia looked at Swarmus. Then she started to shake. For a bright but tiny moment I thought she was trembling with fear.

But she was only laughing.

'You won't activate that device, boy,' Zenia said, her voice horribly distorted through her mutated larynx. 'Even if you knew how to, you lack the stomach.'

'Maybe he does.' Jamila walked over to join me. 'But I don't. You've been in my head – you *know* I don't.' Jam was talking a good fight but I could hear the shake in her voice, feel the sweat in her palm as she held my free hand. 'We'll end this for everyone.'

'Yes, Danny!' Adi called weakly, struggling up on the floor below me. 'Activate it . . . you must activate it . . .'

Then Swarmus opened his grisly mouth. 'The device . . . takes fifty seconds . . . to power down the . . . low-frequency magnetic field.'

I bit my lip. Of course, Swarmus knew everything

that Drone had; he and the transformed Alpha were one being now.

'Fifty seconds is more than enough for me to bond with my subject.' Zenia extended a twitching mantis-arm to Baddi. 'Then, should the antimatter activate, it is of no consequence. Indeed, it will help us! The blast will destroy our bodies but set free our combined digital intelligence.'

'And Swarm intelligence respawns at the last Swarm node,' I realised. 'With the ISS destroyed, that regeneration point will be—'

'Right in the heart of Galactic Swarm M31!' Zenia gloated. 'And we shall tear out that heart . . .'

I looked at Jamila. 'What do we do? She's right – I can't even work this thing. Can you?'

She shook her head and a tear fell down her cheek. 'Throw it down. Maybe it'll explode straight away.'

'Maybe it won't!'

'You *can* activate it, Danny!' Adi yelled up at me. 'You know how, I showed you.'

'Lies,' hissed Swarmus.

'Trust, Danny!' Adi's head fell back, her teeth gritted. I knew I was watching her die. 'That's how I rigged it. Touch! Handhold . . . *TRUST* . . .'

And I remembered Adi squeezing my hand in the passageway deep beneath the concourse. Her fingers on my skin, tapping Morse code.

'TRUST' in Morse code. She'd been prepping me – for this moment! I felt a rush of fear and wonder. *Touch*, she'd said. What did that mean? Maybe the controls were touch sensitive, triggered by the right rhythm. But there *weren't* any controls: none that I could see . . . ?

Baddi gave a sudden gurgling cry. Zenia was crouching over her. Sickly green lights had begun to envelop them.

'The handhold,' Adi shouted again. Swarmus stamped over and kicked her away like a ball of trash. She slammed into the ruins of the information booth.

'What did she mean?' asked Jam, breathless. 'Handhold?'

'She was holding my hand when she tapped out TRUST in Morse,' I whispered, turning over the barbell, trying to trace any buttons. 'I think that's how I switch it on, but where . . .'

'Duh!' Jamila groaned. 'Handhold equals where you're *hold*ing it in your *hand*. The shaft of the barbell!'

'Oh my days,' I breathed. The light show down below was growing brighter and Hulk-green. I saw Baddi's limbs convulse as Zenia's body became glutinous, like some giant pupa breaking free from a chrysalis. *Hold on, Baddi*, I thought, willing her on with all my strength as I tapped at the bar of the containment device. A dash for T, dot-dash-dot for the R, dot-dot-dash for U . . .

My mind went blank.

Jamila must have guessed. 'Dot-dot-dot!' she wailed. 'S! S as in SOS!'

I tapped out the S and added a final dash for the T. Any fears I had about how much pressure to use, or whether the length of my dashes were too long or too short, faded as the barbell started to glow a warning red. It grew hot and I almost dropped it straight away. But Jamila put her hand next to mine, helped me hold on.

'Don't let go!' Adi shouted from the wreckage,

propped up on one elbow with the last of her strength. 'Hold it up – to Zenia!'

'You are too late,' Zenia roared, her body beginning to blend with Baddi's. 'It will take fifty seconds to power down the magnetic field, remember? You cannot stop us!'

'Think so?' Adi actually looked to be smiling now. 'That might be true if we planned to use the electromagnetic field to release the antimatter. But I've rigged that device to work *backwards*. The antimatter will release the electromagnetic field!'

Jamila was succinct: 'Huh?'

'Strong electromagnetic fields damage DNA,' Adi yelled back. 'And there's never been an electromagnetic field like what's coming . . .'

'Powered by antimatter,' I breathed.

'No!' As if suddenly realising the danger she was in, Zenia tried to pull away from Baddi, but the glow was binding them together. Swarmus turned to face us. His fists clenched.

'Hold on, Danny-boy.' Jamila put her other hand on

the barbell, helped me keep the aim. 'I've got you. We've got this.'

Swarmus got ready to jump.

'We've *got* to have got this,' said Jamila. 'Hold . . . *on . . .*'

The monster's clay-grey bulk sprang towards us. And then the barbell erupted in a light storm so intense it shut down my eyes. And I heard Adi cry out—

No. *Sing* out.

In the storm we'd unleashed, in the wild vortex of power, Adi's voice was like a song of triumphant joy.

It was the last thing I knew before my world sparked out completely.

LATER

When light came back to me, it felt like an impossible memory: the most incredible display of high-energy photons cascading all around. I watched a dance of X-rays and gamma rays, patterns and colours beyond my sight. It was like I was seeing creation itself, not with eyes, but with my soul.

Or maybe I was seeing through someone else's mind. Someone whose senses were far more than human.

Gradually the lights faded into a cool and restful dark. I would have been happy to stay in it for days, but now I could feel a hand resting on my forehead.

My eyes flickered open. I was lying in sunlight, back at the Top of the Rock. Confusion cascaded through my thoughts like breeze blocks. 'Have I been dreaming?'

'No, Danny. It was real.' Adi was sitting beside me.

She looked pale, sweaty and weary. 'You were exposed to extraordinary levels of electromagnetic radiation,' she announced. 'But you will heal.'

'Adi . . . ?' I breathed.

She hesitated, looking almost awkward. 'No, Danny.'

'Baddi, then.' I guess my disappointment must have showed.

'I . . . do not appreciate this nickname,' she said slowly. 'My powers healed the radiation damage in you. Healed Jamila. Even to one such as you, with such an illogical sense of good and evil, these are not bad acts.'

'Fair,' I conceded, as I took in Jamila sprawled behind her. 'Sorry. But, Adi – *my* Adi . . . ?'

'I survived too.'

I turned to see Adi kneeling at my other side. It was like that old story about how an angel and a devil sit on different shoulders, tugging your thoughts between good and bad. Or in this case, I suspected, between what was just unlikely and what was surely impossible.

Like: 'How did we get back up here?'

'The flux coordinates were fresh in my mind from

when I placed you and Jamila here before,' said Adi.

'We were almost destroyed in the electromagnetic storm,' said Baddi. 'We were only able to regenerate ourselves by consuming and converting energy from the antimatter blast.'

'Such absorption compares badly with Kung Pao chicken or pizza,' Adi reflected.

'In any case,' Baddi went on, 'we felt it unwise to linger at Grand Central. The people affected by the M-DNA have already begun to recover. They will find much damage to the railway station and seek someone to blame.'

'Don't look at me. I think I'm kind of short to have messed up their ceiling,' said Jamila.

I *did* look at her, and I grinned. 'Glad you made it.'

Jamila raised her head from the floor and waggled her fingers at me. 'Hey, Danny-boy. Welcome to the survivors' club.'

'Again,' I breathed. 'Adi . . . other Adi . . . you know what I'm going to ask.'

'What the hell happened back there?' Jamila

agreed. 'You can tell me too. Just the headlines. Keep it simple, yeah?'

'High intensity electromagnetic fields are bad news for DNA,' Adi began. 'They break down the binding strands within the cells. A big enough field can destroy them completely.'

'And that's what we did with the containment device?' I asked. 'Let rip with an electromagnetic thingy powered by antimatter?'

'Makes sense,' said Jamila unexpectedly. 'They have antimatter engines on *Star Trek*. Gotta be a sound scientific principle, right?'

'I've encountered antimatter-based technology on many worlds as a scout for the Swarm,' said Adi. 'I used that knowledge when repurposing the containment device.'

'Without telling us,' Baddi added.

'Just as well, by the sounds of it,' I remarked. 'If Drone had known, so would Swarmus and Zenia and then . . .' With a shudder, I moved on. 'What happened to the big bads – and to you, Baddi?'

'Or Goodi, right?' Jam corrected me.

'Well, -*ish*. But whatever, *what happened*? You and Zenia were all set to change like Drone did . . .'

'Malusonian DNA is far more susceptible to damage from electromagnetic radiation,' said Adi simply. 'The planet Malus has a strong magnetic field – it has always protected them from their sun's radiation, so they never evolved any defences. While human DNA was merely damaged in the blast, the M-DNA was completely destroyed.'

'So Zenia's dead?' I asked.

'Atomised.' Adi nodded. 'Not a trace remaining.'

'And Swarmus? Uh, Drone, I mean – no, sorry.' I sighed. 'I mean, your partner the agent. Was he zapped along with Zenia? Has he gone back to the Swarm to respawn?'

'Yes. *Now*, he has. His body was *almost* completely obliterated as Alpha was destroyed,' said Baddi. 'But there was enough Swarm code and physical matter left behind for us to trigger his regeneration cycle.'

'And bring his body back to life.' Adi nodded. 'We could not allow his intelligence to migrate back to

Galactic Swarm M31 until we were certain he was free of the Malus mutation.'

'And you *are* certain,' I said. 'Right?'

'Correct,' Adi confirmed. 'The threat from Malus is over.'

Let's hope so, I thought. Sitting up slowly, I stared out over the city through the glass barrier, just as before. Only now the air was busy with TV news and police helicopters, and the sound of sirens rose like ghosts from the streets far below. New York was coming back to life.

It was Jamila's turn for a question and she took the words from my mouth: 'What about everyone Zenia possessed? Will they live?'

'I intend to stay to make sure all trace of the Malus influence is gone from this world,' said Adi, 'and to heal the genetic damage caused in its removal.'

'Eight million people,' Jamila said slowly. 'That's gonna keep even you busy for a while.'

'Wait a sec.' I looked at Adi. 'Does this mean you're staying? Here on Earth?'

She smiled. 'For a time. Right, Goodi?'

'This is why we sent "Drone" back to the Swarm before he could wake properly from his ordeal,' Goodi explained. 'When *I* return, I shall inform the Swarm Sentinels that the threat to Earth from Malus has been neutralised and all improper technology removed. As for Adi, she perished along with Zenia and Alpha.'

Jamila actually gasped. 'You're gonna lie to the Swarm?'

'I believe I have form in this,' she said wryly. 'Since you have been severed from the Swarm, Adi, and since I have replaced you and am considered reliable, no one will come looking.' Goodi gave her a look. 'Use your freedom well.'

'Freedom,' said Adi, and I could tell how sweet the word tasted to her. 'I am grateful, my sister.'

'Sister? Your sentiment is illogical.'

'Spoken like a baddie, Goodi,' I said softly.

'You have to admit,' Jam said, 'that if Adi hadn't thought outside the box – or outside the containment device, anyway – none of us would be here now.'

'I do,' our would-be Goodi admitted. And as she

looked at Adi now, her face actually softened. 'It seems I – *we* – have a weakness for mutation even when not in flesh-being. We allow ourselves to be infected with the ideas of others. With yearnings for what it is to be flesh . . . to have feelings.'

'The Swarm protects and polices all worlds that support life,' Adi reminded her. 'For without life, what is the universe? A dead and empty tomb that lasts forever.'

'Life is a thing to study,' Goodi said, as if reciting some ancient mantra. 'Life is to catalogue. To learn from.'

'The most important thing it teaches us is that change is vital. Inevitable.' Adi smiled. 'Even when it is thrust upon us, change doesn't have to be a bad thing.'

Jamila nodded. 'Just . . . different.'

'And how different is New York to home!' I declared, standing up. I felt surprisingly good. Ready to devour the days ahead of me and all they would bring. 'Home! Oh my days, how am I gonna explain to Mum what I'm doing here?'

Jamila's face clouded. 'Everyone back home's gonna

freak. We don't even have passports!'

'These issues are swiftly remedied,' Goodi said. 'I will unblock the barriers Zenia placed in the minds of those who know you, Jamila. And make your mother believe your visit here was all her idea, Danny.'

'Wait!' Jamila frowned. 'What barriers? What do you mean?'

'Basically everyone's forgotten you existed,' I explained, and her face fell. 'But chill – at least your mum can't ground you!'

'Normality will be restored,' Adi promised her.

'And there are many ways you can travel home with me beside you.'

Jamila grinned. 'Just as long as they involve first-class everythings,' she said. 'Speaking of class, how swanky a place is Mrs Munday putting us up in? Seeing as this trip is all her idea . . .'

I smiled, staring out at the sun nudging down behind the skyline. Yeah, sure, there were details to fix, problems to sort. But we'd get there. All of us taking down the issues together, one at a time.

Maybe one day we'll figure out how to do that as an entire race.

One day.

SCIENCE STUFF

Antimatter: Matter which is very rare throughout the universe and has an opposite electric charge to normal matter. A collision between matter and antimatter results in both being destroyed and a large amount of energy released.

Alpha Magnetic Spectrometer: An experiment mounted on the outside of the International Space Station that measures antimatter in cosmic rays. This helps scientists to understand the formation of the universe.

Digital biosynthesis: The concept of merging biological and digital systems. For example, robots with biological brains, or biological bodies with digital brains.

Fast Radio Burst: An extremely energetic burst of energy, lasting only a fraction of a second. Many FRBs have radio frequencies and, at their source, can release as much energy as the Sun puts out in three days. However, by the time they arrive on Earth, their signal is very weak. At least one FRB has been detected that repeats in a regular way.

Light Year: The distance that light travels through a vacuum in one Earth year. Light travels at almost 300,000 km every second. That's seven and a half times round the world in one second! So in one year, light travels about 9.5 trillion kilometres.

Quantum Computers: Powerful computers which are many times more capable, in terms of speed and processing power, than other computers in use today.

Quantum Entanglement: A weird phenomena of quantum mechanics, in which two particles share the same state, even when separated by extremely large distances. Entangled particles could potentially be used as a means of instantaneous communication over long distances in the future.

Radio Waves: A type of electromagnetic radiation. Radio waves travel through the vacuum of space at the speed of light.

SWARM SPEAK

Bodyprinter: Swarm technology that converts digital code into organic matter.

Dataswarm: A digital superintelligence travelling through space at the speed of light in fast radio bursts. Commonly abbreviated to 'Swarm'.

Digiscanner: Swarm technology that converts organic consciousness (brainwaves) into digital code.

Energenes: Energy genes placed into a biological body by Swarm technology. Energenes provide a source of power that enables quantum 'rolling of the dice' to force an outcome but cause ill-effects in the host.

Flux: A field of energy created when quantum physics is used to 'roll the dice' of possibility and force a desired outcome.

Flux Travel: When energenes are used to bend space and time in order to travel from one point to another. It takes a large amount of energy to flux travel and can only be accomplished over short distances.

Galactic Swarm M31: A dataswarm sent from the Hive Mind in the direction of the Andromeda galaxy, the closest galaxy to the Milky Way.

Guardians: A layer of protection that surrounds the Swarm. Guardians are like antivirus, checking all code that enters the Swarm for malware.

Hive Mind: An ancient alien civilisation forged into a single superintelligence. Approximately sixty-five million years ago, these aliens used quantum computers to transform their biological minds into digital equivalents. From the Hive

Mind, this intelligence has been exploring the universe in dataswarms ever since.

Malus: A planet in the Tau Ceti system. Tau Ceti is a star similar to the Sun and only twelve light years away.

Physical Destructor Code: Code placed by the Swarm into a biological body which, when triggered, causes it to disassemble.

Swarm Agents: Biological machines assembled using Swarm technology. Created when it becomes necessary for the Swarm to interact with physical matter on an alien planet. Swarm agents usually replicate the primary lifeform in a crude, although powerful, form.

Swarm Nanites: Tiny robots assembled from specks of metal dust that can gather material to build larger objects, such as Swarm agents.

Swarm Nation: When lifeforms of lesser intelligence are

translated into the Swarm, a separate Swarm nation is created for that particular species.

Swarm Sentinels: Master code designed to direct and control all activities within the Swarm. Sentinels monitor, analyse and correct any malfunctioning units within the Swarm.

Swarm Scout: Swarm code designed to make an initial assessment of an alien planet. The scout's work is to confirm a planet's situation with the aid of tracker bots and to infiltrate technology, paving the way for Swarm solutions. Adi is the scout for Galactic Swarm M31.

Tracker Bots: Swarm code designed to infiltrate and control existing technology. Tracker bots work with the Swarm scout to observe, monitor and report back to the Sentinels.

Translation: The process of uploading organic consciousness (brainwaves) into digital code.

MORSE CODE

A: • —	N: — •
B: — • • •	O: — — —
C: — • — •	P: • — — •
D: — • •	Q: — — • —
E: •	R: • — •
F: • • — •	S: • • •
G: — — •	T: —
H: • • • •	U: • • —
I: • •	V: • • • —
J: • — — —	W: • — —
K: — • —	X: — • • —
L: • — • •	Y: — • — —
M: — —	Z: — — • •

1: • — — — —	6: — • • • •
2: • • — — —	7: — — • • •
3: • • • — —	8: — — — • •
4: • • • • —	9: — — — — •
5: • • • • •	0: — — — — —

Using the Morse Code alphabet,

can you work out these messages?

(The **/** symbol is used to denote a space between words)

1. – • – • • • – • • • –

2. • – • • – – – • – –

3. • • • • – – • • – – • – • • /
   • • • – • – – • • – – – – •

4. – • • • • • – • – – / • – • – • • /
   – • • • • – – • – • – • –

5. • • • • • – • – – • • • – • • – – •
   – – – • – – • • – •

Morse Code Answers:
1) TRUST 2) ENEMY 3) SPACE STATION 4) THEY ARE BACK
5) SUPERPOWER

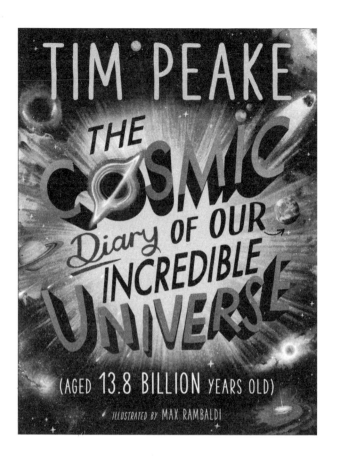

The Cosmic Diary of our Incredible Universe

by Astronaut Tim Peake and author Steve Cole

Get set for mind-blowing adventure through space and time, and understand some of the **REALLY BIG QUESTIONS** about how our incredible universe came to be!